CRY BABY BRIDGE

A COLLECTION OF UTTER SPECULATION

Edited by

LCW Allingham, River Eno and Susan Tulio

To our readers, we are grateful.

Whether you were with us when we were a group of writers collaborating on a project or you've just come on since we've turned that collaboration into Speculation Publications, thank you for your continued support.

In Memory of Patricia Allingham Carlson
August 9, 1956 – September 10, 2023

CONTENTS

CONTENT WARNING

This book contains stories with
suicide, murder, infanticide, miscarriage and
still birth, sexual and physical assault, mental
health issues, spousal abuse, graphic
descriptions of injury and death, loss and grief,
and extreme gore.
For a story specific guide, visit our website.
www.speculationpub.com

Cry Baby Bridge : A Collection of Utter Speculation

FOREWORD

Bridges.

It's not surprising that humans find wild places dangerous and scary. The lonesome heath at night. The whispering, dim forest. The unknowable ocean depths.

Civilization pushes back those wild places. We build roads across the empty places, houses, boats to cross the ocean. Places of safety.

And then we populate our human places with the ghosts and monsters we thought we left behind. How many haunted houses have you run across in books and movies? How many urban legends involve a car and a road trip? How many monsters have thrown their tentacles around a boat in our fiction?

The wild, it seems, will have its way. Fears, that may stretch back to the earliest living things able to feel fear, still linger in our modern minds and squeeze back into our modern world despite all the walls we have built up against them.

Take bridges.

Bridges, like so much of the human-made world, have worked their way into our imagination and our language. "Don't burn your bridges," we say. And, "I'll cross that bridge when I come to it." Bridges have become more than just steel and stone, wood and asphalt. A bridge is a metaphor.

Not every bridge in our imagination is a sad one. Paul Simon's and Art Garfunkel's "Bridge Over Troubled Water" is a bridge of love. With Katherine Paterson's *Bridge to Terabithia* we move into darker territory. And Ambrose Bierce's story, "An Occurrence at Owl Creek Bridge," is all war and death, high suspense and grim tragedy.

The ambiguity of bridges, I think, is there are two ways to look at them. You can see a bridge as a way to cross a daunting river or chasm, to get to some place you'd rather be. A positive feeling.

Or you can pause in the middle and look down, and realize that if you fell, or jumped, death might be waiting below. The French have a phrase: *l'appel du vide*. The call of the void. When you stand on a height and have the sudden urge to jump off. Most of the time, the urge is faint. But it is unexpected and unnerving. Feeling it, we may take a step backward and try to gather ourselves. "What's wrong?" our friend says, seeing us. "Oh, it's nothing," we reply. Most of us resist this urge to self-destruction, most of the time. A few don't.

A bridge is a terrifying thing, if you think about it too deeply. And we haven't even started on the ghosts, yet.

●

Let's take a glimpse at the stories in this volume.

Jeff Provine's "The Legend of Ghost Boy Bridge" starts with another prominent site for ghost stories and urban legends, the lonely road. I love the gritty description of the country road, the bridge, and its sketchy history. (Most of the bridges in this volume have sketchy histories, as you might expect.) Three teens in a car, a ghost, a dare—something is definitely going to go wrong.

"Caroline and the Girl Under the Bridge," by Dori Lumpkin, is story of intertwined lives across time, troubled lives, that meet beneath a bridge. I can't say more for fear of spoiling things, but the story is artful and satisfying.

Ef Deal's contribution to this volume, "Concrete Soul," is a dark hymn to the terrors of childhood and an evocation of the thoughtless cruelties with which adults treat children and children treat each other. It's beautifully written with a pen dipped in acid and truth, and although you might want to, you can't look away.

"This Too Shall Pass" uses the bridge metaphor in two ways at once: the bridge you jump off, and the bridge you cross to get to someplace better. River Eno mixes in ghosts for a twisty lovers' break-up tale.

"What Sort of Woman" is Cat Voleur's tale of mystery, suspense, blood and betrayal. After reading it, you may wonder whether humans are the real monsters.

Derek Heath's remarkable "Time and the Bear" cannot be described, only experienced. Suffice it to say that I am glad I am not Anders, the bear, the bridge or any other character in the story.

"On Patrol At Copperhead Bridge," by Ray Daley, is story full of warmth and local color, told in the charming colloquial voice of a game warden who, with his partner, help in police matters. But the game wardens have a secret.

It's said that writing is easy: all you do is sit down at the keyboard and open a vein. Brent Salish's "Skinning Bone" suggests that making rock and roll is the same, only with guitars.

Jean Jentilet's "Underneath" starts in a place we've been before, but ends up somewhere unexpected. It's a clever meta-story of urban legends about ghosts and bridges.

William J. Donahue's "Hannah's Bridge" employs the classical Unities of Time, Place and Action, as well as William Faulkner's admonition that the only thing worth writing about is the human heart in conflict with itself. By the end, poor tormented Hannah believes she has solved her problem, but I have to wonder whether being guided by a ghost is ever wise.

And there they are, bridges and babies and ghosts. A collection of remarkable tales of suspense, horror, blood, and fear, of human weakness and human strength, of the foggy country where reality breaks down and urban legend begins. I enjoyed these stories immensely, and I'm sure you will, too.

- John Schoffstall, Author of *Half-Witch*, August, 2023

Cry Baby Bridge : A Collection of Utter Speculation

The Legend of Ghost Boy Bridge

Jeff Provine

Ghost Boy Bridge is only six or seven miles outside of town, but nobody comes out this way except during deer season. Most times, people will drive around it to the little wooden bridges out of respect, or fear, of the ghost boy. It's a huge concrete bridge that sticks up from the gravel-and-shale road that turns to dust whenever it hasn't rained for even two days. The bridge stands like a monument, massive and quiet, even though it was built decades before the ghost boy fell there. Your granddad always said the bridge was the product of a county commissioner in the fifties who had a brother-in-law in construction.

You've been there plenty of times, mostly from your older cousins driving you there to scare you while babysitting even though your parents said not to leave the house. You never told on them, no matter how bad the nightmares were afterward.

Driving over the bridge during daytime is bad enough with the eerie quiet of the concrete instead of the rumbling gravel and deep shadows of the trees hanging over the draw. It's worse at night, and tonight is Halloween, the worst night of all. You have goosebumps even before you get into Jessa's old Pontiac Vibe. By the time she stops in the middle of the bridge and switches off the engine, you're shivering inside your pirate costume, holding the plastic hook with both hands.

Everything is quiet.

"So this is it?" Bradley asks from the back seat. His glasses stick out, ruining his pirate costume despite the cape and plastic teeth. He's never been here. His family only moved to town two months ago.

You turn back and put a finger over your lips. "Sh!"

He and Jessa both sit silently staring at you.

You try not to laugh from nervous giggles. "Sorry. I'm not sure why I did that."

"Because we're supposed to hear the ghost, right?" Bradley asks.

Jessa snorts, tossing the tails of her Pippi Longstocking wig. "Oh, new kid, we can't hear him from inside the car. We gotta get out."

She pops the driver's door open with all the flourish of someone who just got her license three weeks ago. "Let's go see if we can really hear him."

Jessa gives her weird narrow-lipped grin that makes her dimples twist up like Pippi would. Then she disappears into the dark.

You turn back to look at Bradley.

He just shrugs.

You shiver again and then hurry out of the passenger door, hoping he thought it was all one movement and you aren't already scared so bad you're shaking.

Out on the bridge, the autumn air is cool. You clutch your poofy sleeves to pull them tight over your arms. When you take a breath, you taste the earthy tones of wood and decay.

There is just enough of the fat crescent moon shining past the cloud-splotched sky to show the outlines of trees and the concrete rails on either side of the bridge. You creep toward the rail, leaning a bit to get a look at the draw below, but after only a few steps, you chicken out and retreat to the car.

Bradley gets out and slams his door. He's looking around, adjusting his glasses with one hand. "Yep, pretty spooky."

You nod. "Totally spooky."

"Cold?" he asks.

You smile at him, bigger than you should, and rub your arms. "Uh, yeah, super-cold tonight."

"It's not too bad," he mumbles. He sticks a hand up. "At least there's not much wind up here in the woods."

"Pfft, you're just trying to be tough." You pause to stick out your tongue. "Jessa, you're cold, right?"

The other side of the car is quiet.

"Jessa?"

No one answers.

You creep around the hood of the car. Warmth radiates from it. You've only been here a second. Where could she have gone?

Just as you round the darkened headlight, a red mass bursts at you with the cry of a banshee leaping from her grave.

You scream and throw your hands over your face for at least a little protection while it mauls you.

It doesn't. It stops and laughs so hard it has to lean over. It's Jessa.

"Oh, ha ha," you mumble.

"Happy Halloween!" Jessa tells you, her face spurting with more laughs. It's all she can muster until she starts giggling again.

Bradley comes around the car from the other side. You cross your arms and turn away. Jessa takes a few deep breaths before she can stand up.

She asks, "Get scared much?"

You stick your tongue out at her.

"I guess that's the reason we came out here, anyway," Bradley says. He turns and stretches while he looks around. "So what's the story of this bridge thing?"

"You think you can handle it?" Jessa asks. Her voice is low now, devoid of laughter.

He shrugs. "Wouldn't be here if I didn't think I could."

Jessa hums. She walks in long, springing steps to the wide concrete rail and sits down on it. She looks up at you. "You want to tell it?"

You shake your head. "No, Jessa, you do it better."

"Fine." Jessa swings her legs up onto the rail beside her. She leans over her knees, eyes wide.

You glance at Bradley. He's watching with his head slightly turned, like he's a scientist studying her. You grit your teeth behind your lips; maybe you should've told it after all.

Too late. Jessa starts, "Used to be, back when there were like three TV channels and nothing better to do, kids would come out to the bridge to hang out. They'd get some booze and crank the car radio and have a party going on. It was perfect since the trees keep the noise down, and there's a long road where you'd see the lights of anybody driving up here."

She points back down the road you came up. You both turn to look even though you had seen it up close just a moment ago. It now seems to run for miles in the dark.

"If it was the cops or somebody's parents trying to break up the fun, everybody at the party can ditch the bottles down in the draw way before they get here."

Now Jessa points over the side of the bridge. She wags her finger, beckoning you to look. With small steps, you follow behind Bradley. You both lean over.

The moonlight can't pierce the deep draw. It's an abyss of total darkness beneath the bridge.

You scoot back.

Bradley takes his phone out, instead. He turns on the flashlight and peers down. "So people don't hang out here now because we have Netflix and actual fun things to do?"

"That, and what happened to Tommy Johnson," Jessa says.

He looks up. "What?"

You smile. "We all grew up hearing it. 'Don't go to that bridge. You know what happened to Tommy Johnson there.'"

"What happened?"

"He partied a bit too hard on Halloween, forty-six years ago." Jessa sighs and shakes her head. "My uncle knew him, said he was a real wild guy who liked to do dares for people. Anything for attention. That night they were having a costume party out here, and he had on this Elvis leisure suit. He started dancing on the rail here with his moves."

She pats the concrete.

You wouldn't dare touch it.

"People were telling him to knock it off, but that just made him do it more. Some people say he slipped. Other people wonder if he wanted to see if he could make the jump, land flat on the water, just to show everybody. Either way, whoosh, off he went."

Bradley looks over the railing again.

"Broke both his arms and his neck in three places," Jessa says, her voice softer now. "He was long dead before anybody could get down to him. They had to bring out firefighters to pull his body up on ropes. But they say his ghost is still down there."

She puts a hand to her ear. "You can hear him groaning at night. And, on Halloween night, like tonight, they say you can see him writhing down there."

Jessa goes quiet. You bite your lips. Bradley doesn't say a thing, just leans farther with his flashlight.

Something groans.

You hug yourself and take another step back.

Jessa jumps up from the concrete and runs to your side. "There it was!"

Bradley hasn't moved. He just keeps studying the darkness and mutters. "Wind, duh."

You point at him. "You said there wasn't any wind!"

"I said there wasn't *much* wind," Bradley says. "Besides, it could be the bridge settling. Concrete expands and contracts, you know."

Jessa hums. "Oh, yeah? If you're so sure, why don't you go down there and prove it?"

Bradley looks up, blinding you for a second with his flashlight before he turns it away. He puts his hand on his hip. "You want me to climb down there to prove to you there isn't a *ghost*?"

"Yeah! Go take a pic with your phone," you cry.

Jessa points to the edge of the bridge where the mossy earth dives into the darkness. "There's the embankment! Go for it, tough guy!"

He chuckles. "Right, and then you two can drive off while I'm down there, so I spend the next hour and a half hiking back home?"

You glance at Jessa.

Her jaw drops. She puts her hands on her hips with outrage. "What? Who would do that?"

You two would. That was the plan. Except, not all the way back to town, but a half-mile, enough that you could swing back around and pick him up. You'd blame the prank on Jessa, talk about how you made her come back, and then you and Bradley would have something to talk about at the party later.

"Give the keys," Bradley says, "and I'll go down there."

Jessa's face flashes with genuine outrage. "Shaw! Like I'm going to give you the keys to my car."

Bradley shrugs. "Whatever. We'll just agree that it's the concrete cooling down then."

Another sighing groan breaks out.

You shiver. "That is totally a ghost."

Bradley extends a hand. "Keys, and I'll check it out."

You look at Jessa. She sneers, but then she digs the keys out of her sweater pocket. She tosses them at Bradley just hard enough he has to catch them with the stomach of his button-up shirt. He fumbles with them and his phone. Then he tucks the keys into his pocket, whips off his black cape and smiles.

"I'll be right back," Bradley sings out. "You guys know that movie, right?"

"Who doesn't?" Jessa snaps.

"It's a good one!" you offer.

Bradley walks away. He hops over the edge of the concrete onto the steep bank. Steadying himself and setting his cape down, he crawls until he disappears.

Jessa stomps and sits on the hood of her car. She crosses her arms.

You sit next to her and shove her shoulder with your shoulder.

"So what's the plan now?" you ask.

Jessa snorts. "It was your plan to start with! I just wanted to go straight to Greg's party, but, no, you wanted to impress the new guy because you think he's cute."

"I do naw—shut up!" Sure, there's no denying it, but at least she could be quiet about it. "It's all ruined now. What are we going to do when he comes back?"

"We could go to the party, like I wanted."

"But…" is all you can manage.

Jessa sighs. "How about when he comes back you help him up the bank? That'll do your 'demonstrate value' and get a jump start on 'engage physically' instead of having to wait to the party."

A loud groan breaks out before you can answer. There are few guttural ticks in it, like the time you yawned too widely in science class and Wayne said he heard it. Your face must have been so red while the embarrassment welded the sound in your mind forever.

"That wasn't concrete," you whisper.

Jessa squeezes her eyes closed. "There's no such thing as ghosts. No such thing."

You swallow.

The groan sounds again, softer this time.

You jump off the car and call out, "Bradley! That's you, isn't it?"

A short, gagging groan is all that answers. Maybe it is him. Maybe he's messing with you. Or maybe he slipped.

You rush to the edge of the bridge where he had climbed over.

Another groan comes, and then another. You see light flashing in the boughs of the leaning trees.

"See?" Jessa says. She has to talk loudly over the groans. "Here he comes!"

"Bradley!" you call again.

The light shines in your eyes. You hold a hand over your face to block most of it out. Around the blinding edges, you can see Bradley's glasses flickering as he lumbers up the bank. You reach down to grab his arm and pull him up to the side of the bridge. He's heavy for such a skinny guy.

"You scared me," you tell him.

Bradley gasps for breath. He leans on you, finally lowering the flashlight. You blink your eyes while you grind your boots against the concrete, trying to support you both. As the fireworks in your eyes disperse, you can make out a shape on Bradley's back.

Jessa screams.

You scream, too, and drop Bradley. He hits the concrete with a thud. Sickening sloshes and the crack of joints ring out as the thing on his back rolls off. It lets out the same terrible groan, now so much louder just a few feet away.

"No," you whisper. You take two steps back and then bolt toward Jessa and the car.

Jessa's already back in the driver's seat. Her hands are waving, and the headlights burst on from her hitting the manual switch.

You dive through the passenger door you left hanging open. Jessa is gasping and swearing. You sit up, putting the thing straight in your view, lit up in horrible glory.

It's a person, at least it looks like one lying on the ground, wearing a yellowed jumpsuit. The clothes are torn and stained brown and red with mud and blood. Then the thing that was on Bradley's back struggles to its feet. It doesn't use its arms; they hang limp at its sides as it leans forward. When it kicks up one knee, the arms swing at jarring angles with the sounds of bone grinding against bone and flesh.

Its head lolls, dangling first behind its shoulder with the face pointed out. When it finally stands, it leans and jerks, tossing its head onto its chest. The dead eyes stare at you from a face with a hanging jaw.

"Tommy," you whisper. In all your years visiting the bridge, you never thought you'd actually see him. It. The ghost.

Bradley sits up behind it. He rubs his head. His glasses stick out, reflecting the headlights to hide his eyes.

"You were right!" he shouts.

You scream. "No, it's just a story! It can't be real! It can't!"

Bradley shakes his head. "You can see him. He…he's lonely. He needs us to join him."

The ghost lets out a terrible groan from its swollen, broken throat. It takes a step toward you, making its arms and head wag and slosh as it goes.

"Crap, crap, crap!" Jessa squeals. She waves her hands at Bradley. "Give me the keys! Gimme keys!"

Bradley just keeps shaking his head. "He's so lonely. He needs us."

It steps toward you again. This time it stumbles. It throws out one arm, trying to catch itself on the hood of the car, but the arm is broken. It lands bodily with a heavy thud.

You look at the struggling ghost, then at Bradley in its shadow, and then at Jessa. Tears are pouring down her cheeks, smearing the makeup dimples she's painted.

You push her out the door, screaming, "Go! Run!"

The ghost groans. It rolls onto its side, the hood of the car creaking and popping.

You don't bother going out your own door. You just crawl across the driver's seat, hitting the horn with your elbow. As soon as your feet hit the concrete bridge, you grab Jessa's hand and run toward the dark road.

You and Jessa run fast, faster than Coach ever could make you no matter how hard she yelled in practice. Jessa's red wig falls off, but you don't even look back for it. You just run until your legs go stiff, and you fall on the gravel road.

No one ever sees Bradley again.

But they say people can see a reflection of light off glasses in the darkness below the bridge when it groans at night.

Carolyn and the Girl Under the Bridge

Dori Lumpkin

2009

Carolyn has a big imagination. That's what they'd said since she was big enough to have an imagination at all. She's good at making up stories, telling people exactly what she wanted them to hear—whatever her version of the truth was. This came in a variety of different forms, beginning with telling her kindergarten grade teacher that her daddy was actually an assassin, and he liked to show her pictures of his victims, and landing somewhere around her and her mom playing spies in the second grade, hiding in the pantry, hoping desperately that the False German Diplomat (Carolyn's daddy) didn't find them and rip their eyeballs out.

The eyeball part was Carolyn's addition.

The False German Diplomat was her mother's.

Carolyn loved her stories. She loved them so much that she pulled them over her eyes like a comfortable blanket, preferring the warmth of the adjacent reality as it compared to the splintered, wooden floors of her own home. They were a pool she could sink into, drowning out the rest of the world by drowning herself in lies.

So when the police finally came, when Carolyn was eleven, asking what had happened and why her mother had been gone for so long, if she was still alive, if she made any reference to leaving at all ever in the whole entire world, Carolyn did what she did best.

She told them her mother was a princess, long-lost and time-forgotten, who left to seek her fortune in Europe. She told them her mother was a pirate, and she went out to sea to find her treasure and would be back, of course she'd be back, to take Carolyn sailing with her in no time at all. She told them her mother was a ghost, had been a ghost all along, and Carolyn herself was half-ghost, didn't you know?

She did not tell them that the man who loomed over her shoulder as she told her stories scared her most of all. She did not tell them that the last time she had seen her mother, the woman was sobbing and telling Carolyn to run, run away and hide.

No, she did not tell them any of that.

1919

There was a lot to be said about the forest that night, the night the soldiers came home. The night Virginia found herself amongst the pines and the stars, hooting along with the owls she had grown up learning to identify. The forest itself was a home to Virginia, twisting walls of branches and a roof of thatched pine straw. She found comfort there.

It was always beautiful. Often, she spent hours in the forest, during the time that everyone else always said could be filled with better things. The empty spaces between laundry, between cooking, between cleaning the home and writing letters to her husband.

Jack.

Her husband, who was home now.

Who was real. Who demanded that she attend to him, instead of spending so much time with her feet in the dirt.

It had been so much easier to love him while he was a soldier; so much easier to carry on a facade she never wanted when it was only letters, only missives meant to keep up appearances. Virginia hadn't prepared herself for what it might've meant when he came home. That the ease of being left alone simply by saying *no thank you, I'm married to a soldier* would transform so solidly into *I am married to a soldier and yes, yes I am so glad he has come home safely to me.*

And, Virginia supposed, she should be a certain modicum of grateful that he did come home. Though it would have been easier if he hadn't. Being a widow always sounded much more appealing than being a wife.

Jack was a good man though, and Virginia was lucky!

She was lucky.

Luck is a funny thing. Virginia thought as she twisted a leaf off of the branch, making her way deeper into the forest. *Luck is the sort of thing that chases you down and tackles you, ain't it?*

It sounded like something her mama would say.

Virginia pressed on, putting more and more distance between herself and the house she came from, where Jack slept peacefully in bed after a full dinner of whatever it was Virginia had cooked. She didn't quite remember. And it didn't quite matter, either. She didn't care much about being a wife. Never had. And, after all, Jack was so simple.

So simple because he had been gone. She didn't need to be a wife, only needed to be the vague idea of taken.

She turned her attention to the path in front of her, following the twisted trail she had been in love with since she was a girl. Except...

She didn't remember it turning that way. She didn't remember those specific trees that now hung above her head, their branches more like a threat than a homecoming. Everything felt so dark; the moon was blotted out. She should have known the way. The path was easy.

Virginia pressed on. Forward into discomfort was better than back inside that house.

As she moved, something low in her gut urged her to keep going, keep pressing on, there was something waiting, please, you're almost there—

Yes.

She stopped.

Before her stood a bridge. A covered bridge, the kind that she had seen in other towns before when she had traveled, but never in her own. Something about it felt old, much older than it looked. It crossed the width of a small mountain river, the likes of which Virginia had also never seen. She frowned. Now was not the time for the universe to play cruel jokes.

The edges of the bridge blended almost perfectly with the path, so that one would never know where the forest itself stopped and the bridge began.

It's as good a place as any, Virginia thought, toeing the edge of the wood.

It was easy for her to come to the decision to stay at the bridge that night. First, it was obviously calling to her for whatever reason. Next, she knew she would never get any sort of sleep with Jack in the bed next to her. She had asked for her own bed, but that was seen as a ridiculous expense. Finally, the forest was her home. It was where she grew up, spent all her spare time and would surely grow old. It was safe here.

It would be safer under the bridge, where any cars or carriages or horses wouldn't see her and assume her dead.

She nodded to herself, satisfied with her decision, before climbing underneath the bridge and into a small divot surrounded by smooth river-stones. It was an almost immediate relief. Her shoulders relaxed, and, for the first time in days, she felt a smile tug at the edges of her lips. Yes.

This was where she belonged.

Let them find her in the morning, if they could at all.

She didn't need to go back.

Virginia let her eyes grow heavy, the ghost of the smile still present on her face.

She was safe here.

2009

What came after the police wasn't fun. They left Carolyn to her stories, casting a disapproving look at her daddy as they left. He said nothing. He always said nothing.

Carolyn didn't know why she didn't leave when her mother told her to. She should have. Should have grabbed her bag and dashed out the door, as fast as she could—faster than she had ever run in gym, or in races against her friends, anything.

But in that moment, when she was watching her daddy at his worst, she stayed put.

The same couldn't be said for when the police left.

He waited patiently until the police had turned off their lights and driven politely away. He watched Carolyn watching them. Whether he could hear her silent plea, her desperate wish for them to return or to take her somewhere else remained unknown, but his eyes bore into her skull with painful precision.

Once they were gone, when the lights dimmed and the evening returned to normal, he looked at her. He looked at her, and he screamed with a fury she couldn't even name.

She ran. First around the house, avoiding his drunken swings, assuming that eventually he would calm down. Eventually, he had to calm down. Eventually, things would return to quiet, and she would return to her room, and her silence and her stories.

When he didn't calm down, when he only got angrier because of her running, the strategy became clear. Get to the door. Get out.

Listen to your mother child, and get out.

So she did.

She ducked and dodged her way past furniture, past shouts, past the life she used to know, darting out the door with the absolute last of her adrenaline.

Later, when she would recount this story to herself, Carolyn would say that she was running from an assassin. A bank robber. That she was a lost princess, just like her mother, and there were people who were trying to take her back to her castle in a kingdom that could never truly appreciate how desperately she wanted to be free.

It was never her father. It couldn't have been. She wouldn't let it be.

But now, she ran.

* * *

1959

Dottie smelled like bubblegum. It was what her boyfriend said he liked best about her, back when his voice was half-muffled, pressed into her chest. He liked bubblegum, and he liked her boobs. He liked the way she dressed, waist all small and skirts all floofy. That's what he called it. *Floofy*. He laughed about it as his hand traveled over her knee, past the petticoats that created the volume, and in deep between apparently bubblegum-scented thighs.

Dottie did not roll her eyes as he did this, though she really really wanted to. It was one of her secret dreams, to tell him that he was an idiot, and she was only dating him because her friends told her it would be good for her reputation. He was, they were right, but god, was it a bit much to suffer through.

And suffer she had, for a long eight months, making the exact right decisions and saying the exact right words. She was happy! Sort of. She didn't mind it, at least. It worked in her favor, and she loved a free dinner. The guy wasn't half-bad looking either, and every so often she could entertain his kissing and fondling and jokes that made her feel a little on the wrong side of uncomfortable.

His hand pressed against the thin fabric of her underwear, and she jumped.

No.

That was too much.

Dottie pulled away, smacking his hand out from underneath her skirt.

"Have you tried asking first?" she snapped, smoothing out the light blue fabric.

He laughed.

"Why would I need to? You're my girl, aren't you?" He pushed towards her again, arms out. Hands grasping. He was like a child.

Dottie grimaced.

"Basic respect, I think?" she replied, rolling her eyes. Her fingers wrapped around the handle to the car door, and she pushed it open. "If you're going to treat me like that, I'll just walk myself home."

He glared at her as she stepped out of the car. It wasn't a long walk, just through the woods and down the street.

"If you leave, I'll tell everyone at school how easy you were. They'll all know you're a whore!"

It was a loosely thought-out insult, and not one she particularly took to heart. She slammed the door in his face.

In moments, his car was on again, engine rumbling as he sped away from the little trail's parking lot. He was gone, and Dottie was alone.

Alone was different. Alone was scary, and dark and harsh.

Before she could stop them, fat, hot tears began to spill from her eyes and roll down her face. They were messing up her makeup, but she couldn't be bothered to care.

Home was close. She could do it on her own, then.

Dottie took off through the woods.

It took her about fifteen minutes of frustrated walking until she finally admitted to herself that she was lost. Painfully lost, it must have been, because she didn't even recognize where she was. She didn't like the woods, per se, but she knew them well enough to travel through them. Not that night though, it seemed.

It wasn't long before Dottie stumbled across a river, and spanning it, a lovely little covered bridge. It looked like the perfect sort of place for a picnic, if it hadn't been ten in the evening and Dottie's relationship hadn't taken a sudden, gross turn.

A shadow moved in the corner of her vision, and Dottie jumped.

It was just a woman. A pretty woman with straw-colored hair in a long braid and a dress that was faded and old, but looked pretty simple. It was long and cotton, like the sort of nightgown that Dottie's grandmother might've worn.

"Who are you?" Dottie squeaked, wiping tears from her cheeks in an effort to seem somewhat normal. The woman looked taken aback, as if she hadn't expected Dottie to even see her.

"Virginia," she responded, her voice wispy and quiet.

"Your dress is old," Dottie said to the woman named Virginia.

Virginia laughed.

"I've been here a long time," Virginia responded, looking at her. "Why were you crying?"

Dottie groaned.

"My boyfriend. Or, I guess he's not my boyfriend anymore, is he? He's just a complete pig." Dottie felt the tears well up again. "I don't understand why they're all like that!" The tears burst, staining her cheeks in the same tracks she had just wiped clean.

"Do you want a hug?" Virginia asked. Dottie nodded, almost desperate.

She moved towards Virginia, who already had her arms out.

"You can stay here a while, if you want. I wouldn't mind the company."

Dottie considered. On the one hand, she could continue on, could go home and face school the next day, everyone calling her a whore and listening to that son of a bitch. They would all hate her, depending on what he said to them. It would be a miserable existence, from then on out.

She really didn't want to do that. She really didn't *have* to go through all that.

The other hand was looking much more comforting.

Dottie nodded slowly, and Virginia smiled. They sat down together at the edge of the riverbank, right underneath the bridge itself. Dottie leaned her head on Virginia's shoulder and cried. It wasn't the same angry sort of sobbing that came before. It was a release. She felt comforted. She felt cared for.

Somehow she knew, deep in her heart.

She was safe here.

●

2009

In her stories, the woods took more forms than Carolyn could count. They were one of the things she particularly loved because there were so many amazing stories about the woods. It was story after story, and each one of them was more perfect than the last.

The first one it had ever been was that the woods were a labyrinth, like she had read in that one library book about all the gods and monsters. It was easy to get lost in them, but if you had the right sort of mindset, or a specific golden thread, you could find the special treasure in the middle of the trees and that would set you free.

After that, it became that the woods were a spy base that Carolyn herself was sent to infiltrate. It was the perfect job for Agent Carolyn, of course, because she had a photographic memory and knew the entire layout by heart. She would never get lost, and could get in and out like an expert, finding and extracting the secret government documents without any trouble.

But now the trees were just trees. Running faster than she ever had before, powered by nothing other than adrenaline and fear, the woods were just woods. There was no labyrinth, no spy base, no castles or princesses or pirates.

She ran until the trees cleared and opened up, spitting her out at the edge of a river. Just a river, not an ocean to sail or the secret home of mermaids.

Resting at the edge of the river though, was a bridge. A covered bridge, the likes of which she had only ever seen in books.

Carolyn stopped running.

Something about the bridge was calling her. The wood seemed old and right. Not like the splintered floors of the home her daddy had spent so much time chasing her around. She knew it held memories. This was a good story-bridge.

Carolyn moved forward, letting the bridge do its job. She pressed on, doing her best to explore and pretend. Same as she always had.

1989

It was late and Jennifer was tired. God, she was so tired. The world was too much, and she was over it. It was all pressure, you know? Pressure from classes, pressure from her parents, pressure to get a job. It all felt so heavy on her shoulders, and it was no wonder she ran herself out into the forest that night.

Nothing really happened to incite the moment, more than the usual. Her mom telling her she needed to move out. Her dad telling her she wasn't doing as much work as her brothers.

She was working so fucking hard.

It was on them that they refused to see it.

Their loss, Jennifer supposed.

She made her way through the woods, trudging past trees and walking steadily to the beat of the music playing through her Walkman. It was a comfort within all the sadness. She could lose herself in music, in the beat that someone else provided for her to live her life by.

She was looking for the river. She knew it was here, it had been there since she was a little girl. The bridge was a comfort to her, a place where she often lost hours, reading or doing homework or any other number of things.

She didn't know what she had been planning on doing once she got there. Killing herself? That didn't feel quite right. Jennifer knew she had a lot to offer the world, and her parents not being able to see that wasn't *her* fucking fault.

She just wanted to get lost for a little while. Lost in the woods, lost in her own thoughts, lost in the way that no one else would ever be able to understand.

And then be entirely fine and continue to work herself to the bone the next day.

Or maybe not.

All things considered, it probably wasn't best for her to do that.

For a moment, Jennifer considered just remaining in the woods, making a home and living there for the rest of her life. It was a silly little dream. An impossible dream, but the idea was fun.

She eventually reached the river and the bridge and felt her entire body relax. This was where she belonged.

Except, something was different that night.

A younger girl sat at the edge of the riverbank just underneath the bridge itself. Her knees were pulled up to her chest with her arms wrapped tightly around them. Jennifer fought the urge to tell the girl to go away. This was *her* riverbank, and *her* bridge, and dammit she didn't want to be disturbed. Except the girl didn't look hardly older than sixteen, and something felt different about her altogether. Something about the way her reddish-brown hair curled in a ponytail at the nape of her neck—or maybe it was the way she didn't seem to be crying, but just sort of contemplating the water—made Jennifer want to pay attention.

She turned off her Walkman.

A stick crunched under her foot. They both jumped, and the girl at the water spun to face her.

"Sorry," Jennifer whispered, almost entirely on instinct. "I didn't mean to disturb you. I come here a lot, I just—"

"You didn't disturb me." The girl smiled, standing up. "I was just..." She motioned to the water. "You know."

Jennifer nodded. She did know.

"You don't really seem like the sort of person who would spend a lot of time in the woods looking for answers."

The girl shrugged.

"Neither do you," she responded.

Jennifer couldn't argue with that. She was a little out of place, considering it was June, and she was wearing a sweater. The girl, at least, was dressed more appropriately in a light blue dress that looked like it walked straight out of the 50s.

"I'm Jennifer." She took a step forward. The girl smiled, moving to the side so that Jennifer could join her by the riverbank.

"Dottie."

They sat down together.

"Hope you don't mind the company, Dottie." Jennifer picked up one of the rocks that lined the bank, turning it over in her hand. "I like to come here to clear out my brain."

"I don't mind," Dottie answered, wrapping her arms around her knees again. "What's wrong?"

"Nothing I can really get into."

Dottie nodded slowly, placing a gentle hand on Jennifer's shoulder. It was sweet. Something about Dottie, about being underneath the bridge with someone who was silent but understood, made her feel like she was actually healing.

Like there wasn't any pressure, and she didn't need to worry about what was going to come next, or about her future, or her job or anything at all. That place, that moment, was secure. Was trustworthy.

Jennifer was proud of herself.

"How long were you going to be here?" Jennifer asked.

Dottie looked at her, a curious expression falling across her face.

"I don't know, not much longer maybe. Until I've got answers. You don't mind, do you?"

"No," Jennifer responded, "I don't mind."

She really didn't.

A flash of a thought passed through Jennifer's mind. A little thought, really, but one she liked. One she took a lot of comfort in.

I could stay here a while.

And she could. She was safe there.

2009

Under the bridge, there was a confusing woman. She was the sort of woman who seemed like she might be in Carolyn's stories, except she was there, and she was real, and she was looking at Carolyn with that same sad, longing expression her mother used to make whenever her daddy had one of his bad nights. She wore a brightly-colored sweater, with big black triangles on it, and jeans that fastened high at her waist. Her hair was brown and frizzy and piled all up at the top with a floofy sort of hair tie.

Carolyn couldn't help but feel like this woman knew something about her.

"I've been waiting for you," the woman said.

"You don't even know me," Carolyn replied.

The woman laughed, holding out her arm, silently asking for Carolyn to join her, to come underneath the bridge too. Something pulled inside Carolyn, and with it came the assurance that yes, she could be comfortable there.

"You're not going to hurt me, right?" Carolyn knew better than to trust the woman's answer, but she wanted to ask anyway. Just to see.

The woman sighed.

"You've been hurt a lot, haven't you?" she asked, her voice still just as calm as the rest of her.

Carolyn bristled.

"No I haven't." She frowned. "Actually I'm perfectly fine, and my daddy is just off the trail waiting for me, so I'd better go."

It was another little test to see what the woman would do. She didn't move. Neither did Carolyn.

"He isn't, is he?" the woman eventually asked.

Carolyn shook her head.

"He probably isn't even looking for me," she admitted, taking a step forward. The woman's hand was still outstretched.

Carolyn took it. The woman pulled her forward, embracing Carolyn in a way that reminded her of her mother. The woman even sort of smelled the same. Like faint violets and old libraries.

Carolyn let herself get pulled under the bridge, coming to rest in a small nest of stones. It was like the spot had been made perfectly for her. Once she was there, she couldn't imagine herself anywhere else.

"You're safe here."

Carolyn believed her, taking the words and using them as a blanket, just as she always had. She shut her eyes. The adrenaline left her body.

She was safe there.

Concrete Soul

Ef Deal

Sol mi, sol mi.

A simple minor third. At 7am, your mother calls you to wake you for school. At 6pm, your mother calls you to dinner. Doesn't matter how many syllables in your name, it's the same minor third, the echoes of your first lullaby cooed throughout the day, soothing, begging you to trust the ones who feed and nurture you, who hold your hand as you take your first steps.

Sol mi, sol mi.

And your soul soars.

At least for the moment. At least for a few short years until the chant is appropriated by the herd of children around you who give you new names in that minor third, wedging it into your soul to give you a new "me":

Tattle-tale, tattle tale! Stick your head in a garbage pail!

Made you look, you dirty crook! Stole your mother's pocketbook!

Nanny Nanny Poo Poo filled your pants with doo doo!

Nyah nyah nyah nyah nyah nyah!

Neener neener neener!

In every culture, every country, a universal call, a primal invocation, a concrete cry cementing your identity to all the world until the next rite of passage. First Communion, first day of school, first time you wet your pants in school…

For the children of Oakland Avenue, the only rite of passage that mattered was the crossing of the ancient railroad bridge with Mrs. Easton when you turned five years old.

Oakland Avenue teemed with children, most of the families being Catholic. No waiting to be picked for a team; someone always grabbed your hand and pulled you into the game of the night and told you where to stand, and you had half the entire neighborhood on your side. You were safe, needed, wanted, and cheered on unless the herd turned suddenly feral, surrounding you, pointing, *neener neener neener! Sol mi, sol mi!* until the mothers of Oakland Avenue leaned out the back doors and chanted your names in a minor third, the ritual that called you all home to be fed and loved.

Every summer evening at 6:30, Mrs. Easton, the Methodist Sunday School teacher, came out to "set" on her front steps and watch the herd playing in the street. Kickball or softball teams comprised David and Nancy; Debbie, Billy, and Tommy; Billy, Eddie, Patty, Peggy, and Theresa; Chucky and Arn; Charlie, Louanne, Franny, and Joe; Ronnie and Lynnie; Margie, Donald, and Kennie; Dale, Dean, Dane, Dianne, and Donna. You. When you saw Mrs. Easton, you'd all finish up the game and gather around her, and she'd listen to your news, your stories, your dreams. She fed your hopes and nurtured your greatest desires.

The herd became Mrs. Easton's flock.

Then at 6:55, she shepherded all of you who were at least five years old into a defile and off you trekked up Oakland Avenue, then turned left on Graisbury. Here, your heart began to beat a little faster. You could smell the sweat of the herd, even if you weren't quite aware of it, a sour tang that told the tale of the day's play as much as the nervous dread of the ceremony to come. A vague shadow loomed a half block up on West Atlantic, a wall of concrete and iron, the first hint of the dark violence of the world just beyond the leafy trees that shaded your walk. The railroad bridge. You laughed harder and talked louder trying to avoid the inevitable moment of decision until it was upon you:

If you were a whiner, a crybaby, a fraidy-cat, you continued up West Atlantic, gathering clover and Queen Anne's lace into bouquets that would invariably die before you could get them home again, trying to ignore the chant of the herd:

Crybaby! Crybaby! Poke you in the eye, baby!

But if you were brave enough, you'd cross the monumental bridge over the railroad tracks to the bank of East Atlantic, to meet up with all the fraidy-cats at the railroad crossing two blocks later, to continue on together to the drug store for snowballs.

You knew nothing of metaphors, but you understood at a visceral level the significance of your passage over that bridge, a ceremonial declaration of your spirit, your fortitude, your honor and your courage. Looming larger than the bridge, the weight of the shame that would smother you if you failed.

Don't you wanna die, baby?

Many times, a new five-year-old would attempt the climb only to run back to the safety of the West Atlantic bank, clasping the hand of Debbie, Billy or Tommy, who never took the bridge even though they were older and probably weren't really afraid because they were bigger. Wasn't there some measure of courage for the ones who didn't cry but strode defiantly away from the leering dare of those concrete steps?

Timing was crucial. The passenger rail, a sleek, silver snake of windowed cars, haggard faces pasted to the glass, some of whom you recognized as neighbors, fathers, passed by at 6:50, but at 7:13 the freight train from Atlantic City came through. So you dawdled up Graisbury Avenue, collecting pretty stones and dandelions, showing off your treasures to Mrs. Easton, vying for her attention and affection and approval until the moment that separated the worthy from worthless.

Far in the distance, the bellowing cry of the oncoming black steel dragon struck fear into your soul.

For five years you'd heard that wail in the night, felt the house shake as the roar closed in on you, cursing you, threatening you, filling your body with horror as the volume drove a scream out of you, then fading away, mocking you as you shoved your face into the pillow and soaked it with tears.

The dragon called you. You quailed. Your skin turned to gooseflesh. Your head rang with the echoes of a taunting minor third. *Sol mi, sol mi.*

Crybaby! Crybaby! Poke you in the eye, baby!

Was it anger that drove you? Was it the desire to be accepted by the herd? You were five; you didn't know.

The bridge...Massive, formidable, but not indomitable. All of the others had conquered the bridge. You could, too. The bridge would keep you above the dragon. The walkway would hold you high and you would look down on the dragon in triumph, maybe a slight sneer of disdain. You would never fear anything again.

The bridge stood as a testament to FDR and the CCC; you had no idea what that meant, but it was engraved on the concrete foundations. Concrete steps, wrought-iron rails a kid could poke a head through or sit and dangle legs over the edge, as the older ones would do.

A foot on the first step announced your commitment to crossing to the world. You couldn't back down unless you wanted that sing-song slap in your ears all the way to the drug store, maybe all your life.

Don't you wanna die, baby?

You set your foot to the concrete. Something like electricity zapped up your whole leg, and you froze for a moment until the predatory toothy grins of the feral herd surrounded you like hyenas, ready to chant. So you wrapped your hand around the rusting wrought-iron rail and pulled yourself up to the next step, then the next. The weight of the concrete, dragging you down at first, became lighter as you climbed. The surge rose to your belly and then to your head with each step. Ten steps to the landing, oh so high, higher than you've ever climbed. What if you fell? But you couldn't fall, and you couldn't stop to fail.

Six steps up to the walkway. Breath came faster and faster, and standing finally at the top step you could see over all the rooftops in town. You laughed and laughed because you really wanted to scream in terror. You clung to the rails, rust staining your clothes and biting into your hands as you watched Debbie, Billy and Tommy on the bank of West Atlantic gathering their bouquets, unashamed, unafraid—safe.

Two blocks away, the railroad crossing bells clanged. Fear exploded in bombs of sweat in your armpits. Red lights flashed, and you clenched your knees tight against the threat of wetting yourself. In the distance, the light of the locomotive glared like the single eye of a steel monster bearing down on you, relentless. If you ran, you could have made it across the bridge before the train got to you. But if you ran, the chant would begin, so you wrapped both arms around the corroded iron, reeling head pressed between the rust, vision blurred as the dragon's one eye blazed and flared. It barreled toward you, just you, because it knew you recognized its power over you and hungered for the taste of your terror. Huge box cars marked with arcane spells heaved toward you. Any second, coming for you, ramming into you...

Then you screamed. The locomotive roared beneath you. You stared in wonder as it disappeared between your legs, beneath the concrete. For the next eighty seconds, the dragon belched fire, the bridge rattled, and the rust grated your skin, and you screamed such a cry that emptied your whole body, that filled you with hilarity.

You lived. You survived. You stared into the faces of the herd, as white and sweaty as your own, and you laughed and laughed, shrill and too sharp.

At 7:15, Mrs. Easton walked serenely across the bridge and down the steps on the other side, her flock safe behind her, and you laughed all the way to the drug store. Syrupy snowballs froze the memory inside you, your courage branded on you for all to see.

Every evening, every summer, you climbed the concrete steps.

Until you were old enough to find new meaning in that old bridge. Long after the herd, long after the 7:13. Night would fall, the street lights would flicker on, and mothers called their children home. *Sol mi, sol mi.*

You weren't a child anymore.

Your first period. Elementary graduation. Your first bra. Junior high with its new cruelties. Your first dance, the scent of the herd pervasive, fear now mingling with a predatory curiosity. Your first broken heart. No Mrs. Easton. Just you, alone. Defiant. Unafraid, unashamed. You survived.

The rusted-wheel grating of the crickets sang a song of endings, with the monotone buzz of cicadas grumbled discontent. Summer was almost gone, and a new rite of passage awaited. You feared nothing. You believed you could survive anything as you sat on the concrete walkway with legs dangling between the rust-red railing posts waiting for the 9:25 train, dropping dandelions and daisies one by one to the tracks below, gazing into the night to catch the dragon's single eye. You were old friends, you and the dragon. Respected adversaries. You had defeated it night after night, year after year, and you never once wept.

"What are you doing here?"

Tommy. So much bigger than you. The cuter brother, smooth brown hair and blue eyes. Football, baseball, wrestling... nothing you ever liked, but you always liked his smile.

In the distance, the dragon announced its advent.

"Waiting for the train."

He scoffed. "Up here?"

You turned away. "You never did like the bridge."

He held out his hand. "Come with me. I'll show you a better place to watch from."

The dragon called again. It knew. The dragon had seen so much more than you could ever know about rituals and passage and the importance of knowing which challenges to face. Its angry roar almost stopped you: *Noooooo...You're miiiiiiine...*

But you had conquered the bridge so many times, and Tommy offered a new challenge, a leering dare. So you took his hand, a commitment to crossing. You followed him down the concrete stairs, below the concrete stairs, under the concrete stairs. You didn't know, couldn't have known what the dragon already knew. Paralyzed as he slammed you into the foundation and clamped one hand over your mouth while the other fumbled to pluck bouquets...

Breath came faster, and you tried to protest. He pinched your nose. No sound but the dragon's roar, summoning you to be brave, challenging you to defy, and you did defy but you failed. Your scream leached into the concrete, deeper than blood, deeper than shadow. It clawed its way up the corroded rails as the train barreled toward the bridge, deafening in metallic blasts, soul-scathing in steel shrieks, arcane symbols cursing you as the cars loomed loud, coming for you. The locomotive bellowed, ramming the breath from you.

The keening of the dragon faded into echoes.

Tears streaked your white face. Life left your body. You saw only his sneer as he zipped and his foot just before he kicked your head into the concrete.

"Crybaby."

Your silence released you, freezing you to the moment as no snowball could do. You fade into the night, into the darkness, beneath the weight of shame.

Sol mi! Mothers call their children home. They will always call.

Sol mi! The herd taunts. They will always taunt.

Years swallow your memory. The foundation devours your flesh. Rust corrodes your bones. Clover and Queen Anne's lace flourish around you like lush tresses of hair plucked by generations of the defiant, the unashamed.

Every evening at 7:13, Mrs. Easton's granddaughter stands with a new flock on the bridge. The dragon roars above their cries, seizing their voices and dragging them into the distance. Their laughter fixes forever their triumph. The bridge shudders beneath their feet, reverberating with Tommy's final curse.

And yes, you cry. You will always cry. You'll never stop crying, your soul cemented forever in a final passage.

Every evening at 7:15 Mrs. Easton's granddaughter pauses, startled, on the concrete walkway, looking back once more, uncertain, before descending the concrete stairs.

This Too Shall Pass

River Eno

Washington's Crossing Historic Park was a short hour and a half from where we lived, but I'd never had the pleasure. We almost never camped so close to home because Erik and Jax needed a challenge to their camps, like steep rock climbs or deep falls—things they couldn't get in the smaller parks closer to the city. Amelia's only requirement was a body of water she could swim in; easy to manage since the Delaware river's restoration project, swimming was now an absolute pleasure.

I loved hiking, steep or flat, long or short, desert or forest, but regardless of our passions, Jax and I couldn't wander too far from the city as the hospital had us on standby for the holiday weekend. There was a high chance, between the marathoners and the fireworks, we'd be called in to work.

The first night I left my tent because I heard a woman crying. It was also the first time camping, in a very long time, that Erik wasn't with me sleeping and snoring or with his foot touching mine. I was wide awake. It was early summer, nighttime chilly in the woods, and I was alone.

A year had come and gone since Erik and I were each other's one and only, but we had all camped together long before Erik and I were a couple; the yearly camping trip being my idea to begin with.

The pain Erik inflicted the night he left me, the way he left, and the subsequent five months after, when, "for his own mental health," he barely spoke to me, was some of the worst loneliness I'd ever experienced. Maybe that's why I was so willing to pretend it was all over, and why I'd come on this trip. It was certainly why I was still awake well past midnight and following the sound of someone sobbing in the woods.

The night smelled of fresh rain, damp earth, and the detritus felt spongy under my boots. The air was still. The crickets were only just emerging, their song not yet overpowering but soothing to the ears and mind. The moon was in its new or dark phase, but I'd been working last-shift most of my working life— all-night gas station attendant, bartending, and now as paramedic—so I wasn't fazed by the blackened quiet. The darkness held a comfort for me the daylight hours couldn't provide.

The main road was winding and partially graveled. My footsteps crunched in the silence until I came upon the Van Sant bridge. A young woman stood halfway through, clutching a bundle in her arms as if holding a baby. She was crying. Her hair was dark and moving in a breeze I didn't feel. I could see her easily because the moon was full, and the sides of the bridge were open…except, a moment ago, there was no moon, and I could have sworn the bridge was fully enclosed when we drove into the park.

She looked to her left, away from me, as if she'd heard something. She gazed at the bundle again, her chest stuttering from crying…and then she was standing on the open ledge. I hadn't seen her move. She was just suddenly standing on the ledge, gripping the blankets to her chest. She took a deep breath and then pitched herself forward and into the water.

Air caught in my throat when I tried to scream, and I choked. "Wait!" I finally called.

My work boots pounded the old creaking planks, echoing under the roof. I stopped where she had been standing, looked over the ledge into the water and saw nothing but a patch of black river.

"Fuck!"

The moonlight receded. The sides of the bridge covered over with boards, fading back into place like a movie effect, leaving me in full darkness save one small, dim lightbulb hanging in the middle.

Something skimmed the top of my head. Many sets of bare feet and the hems of nightgowns swayed from the old rafters.

"What the fuck?"

I backed up, stumbling into the side, then ran off the bridge. The sky was black. No moon. The bridge was empty, sides closed tight. No woman. No bodies.

I shook a shiver up my back. I'd seen some weird shit, but that was by far the weirdest.

The next day I crossed the bridge at least fifteen times looking for any sign of the apparition or hanging bodies. Erik and Jax decided I'd imagined it because it was late, and we'd had a few drinks before we went to bed. I was beginning to doubt myself, but Ameila believed me. She believed in all the supernatural things they made podcasts about.

"See, I told you!" Amelia pulled back the foliage covering the sign on the opposite end of the bridge. "This is a Cry Baby Bridge!"

I frowned as I read, I didn't remember her telling me anything about it. "One of many bridges around the world where the sound of a mother or baby crying can be heard from the bridge or water below…"

I'd never even remotely heard of this phenomenon. If Amelia did tell me, maybe the story got lodged somewhere in my subconscious, and I did imagine it.

"The legend of this bridge has it that the mother gave birth to a stillborn baby, and in her grief threw herself into the river so they could be together." Amelia sighed. "Isn't that just horrible? To see no way out of your sadness you want to die. My aunt always said suicide was a permanent solution to a temporary problem."

That seemed like a simplification or invalidation of the human condition. I could relate to feeling so sad that I'd do anything to not feel that way. I hadn't thought of hurting myself specifically, but I had thought that if I wasn't here, I wouldn't feel so awful anymore. I turned my head away, not wanting Amelia to see the pain rush into my face. After a year, that level of emotion, for something I was supposed to have moved on from, was embarrassing.

"It says, for this particular bridge," Amelia continued. "You can hear the woman on calm, dark nights crying for her lost baby."

"You can see her as well," I said. "Unless that was just a nauseatingly awful perk for me."

"I'm sorry, Piper. That must have been terrible." Amelia squeezed my hand and then gave me a small smile. "But also, that is really freakin' cool!"

"It really wasn't. And the sign says nothing of anyone hanging themselves from the rafters. But I'm telling you, that's what I saw."

Why was it that memories from the middle of the night faded quicker than most, their edges softening to nothing the harder you tried to remember details.

"No, nothing about any hangings," said Amelia, her nose stuck in her phone searching. "But my service is sketchy."

I shrugged. I had never lost a baby, but I was relating to this woman…or these ghosts. I wore their grief like it was my own. To have something you loved so much, something you gave everything to, only to have it ripped from you by a will beyond your control was insanely unfair and heart smashingly fucking painful. How exactly was a person to get over such a loss?

Another cross of the bridge, and Amelia pulled me away for lunch and a group walk around the lake. At the beach Erik was lagging, as usual, then came from behind Jax and I, heading toward the dock. I automatically reached out to take his hand, stopping myself just before our fingers touched. I doubted anyone saw it, but I put my hand in the other, rubbing them together as if I were chilly and not humiliated.

"Partner up," said Amelia that evening, after dinner, as we cleaned the campsite.

"Must we," Jax said, "with the charades? Every single time."

"I love charades," I said, filling the food bucket with plate scrapings.

"That's because you and Erik always win!" Jax practically yelled.

"Damn straight!" I laughed. "And we can do it again, can't we?"

"Guys against the girls," said Erik, averting his eyes. "That'll be fun."

"Yeah, sure." I forced a smile and nodded. "That's cool."

"Finally," said Jax, "I have a chance."

"Yay!" Amelia laughed. "I'll go get my notebook to keep score."

Amelia and I won. I should have felt good about that, snarky even, like Erik must be regretting not playing with me. But all I felt was squashed that Erik couldn't stand to be my partner for a simple two-hour game of charades.

My walk, late in the night, took me to the bridge, looming like a giant black hole in the shadowy forest; the small, dim, yellow bulb accentuating the depth of the chasm. I stared into it for what felt like an eternity, my heart heavy, almost yearning, for someone I didn't know, someone who hadn't been alive for centuries, afraid if I stepped back onto that bridge, I'd step into a past that wasn't my own...and yet somehow was my future.

●

I woke around noon, rolling over in my double sleeping bag to empty space. I closed my eyes, trying to gain control over the ache in my chest. I took a deep breath of cool morning air, flattening my palms on the grass to feel the grounding energy soak into my skin. When I was calm, I dressed and crawled out of my tent.

The chairs were set up around the fire pit from last night. The coals were hot, and the coffee pot was on a small table set to the side. Erik and Jax were gathering their gear for a soft climb.

"Hey," I said, stretching to stand.

"Good morning," said Jax, glancing up with a smile.

I walked to the firepit, looking for the breakfast pans. "Any food leftover?"

"Of course." Amelia handed me a full plate. "I put it aside before the only thing left was bread."

"Thanks." I gave her a weak smile.

In the past it was Erik who would make sure I didn't get cheated with breakfast.

I sat by the fire, plate on my lap and poured my coffee. Erik threw his pack onto his back and started through the woods without a word. Jax followed. "Have a good morning, fellow campers," Jax called over his shoulder.

Amelia emerged from her tent in her bathing suit and with a small rucksack on her back. She smiled. "I'm going to swim with that cute girl I met yesterday."

I swallowed my food and nodded.

"Oh." She turned around when she hit the trail. "I put the dirty dishes in the wash basket. I gave you breakfast clean-up duty. I mean, that was all that was left, so you got it." She started up the trail toward the other campsite.

I was immediately sullen. I didn't mind being alone or kitchen clean-up. I usually ended up with it as I slept late. But it used to be Erik would hang back and spend a bit of time with me before he left for a climb. Now, I just felt disregarded whenever he's around.

Rationally, I didn't really want to still be coupled with Erik. If he could leave me the way he did, I was better off. It was just so much change, so much damage, so abruptly…like the mother, pregnant one day, empty the next. It was hard to catch up and be normal. Whatever that was. But I did once have a normal, and I longed for it.

Nothing changed until everything changed. That's what my aunt used to say.

I ate breakfast while checking my phone. My sister emailed again about her visit, the one I kept putting off. The idea of a house guest, even my sister, overwhelmed me. Noah texted me about twenty-five times since I'd left. A bunch were questions about the ghosts. I'd messaged him that first night, when I got back to my tent. The last three texts were pictures of the empty side of our ambulance. On the seat he'd placed a small doll made from a dried potato and wearing a black conical hat. It made me smile. If he had come, he would have stayed behind to keep me company. He was kind, a good work partner. But I wasn't in the mood for conversation, so I didn't answer any of his questions.

I washed the dishes in the river, cleaned my hoodie of yesterday's food splatters, collected water to boil for lunch and chopped extra firewood for the evening. I was hanging the sweatshirt on the line I'd strung from my tent to the nearby tree when I heard Jax's laughter coming from the trail. Before I saw them, I grabbed my pack and left for a hike. I was still irritated and didn't want to show it.

I texted Amelia when I was far up the trail heading toward the bridge to let her know I'd be hiking for a few hours. I didn't want to leave my dinner plate up to Erik. It wasn't his job. Not anymore.

●

I walked the river's edge, the anguish projected from the tormented ghosts eating away at my heart. I told myself ghosts weren't real. They were stories around a campfire or at a sleepover when you were twelve. Amelia believed, because her mom believed and so on. No one ever really saw them...except that I did. I could still feel the phantom of their dour energy coating my skin. Surreal is what ghosts are, but I couldn't deny it was the most real thing I'd ever seen.

As I walked the area around the bridge, a familiar ache twisted deeper. The weight of those lost souls rested on top of my own pain. Scenes of the woman jumping with her baby tight in her arms and then falling into the cold, dark river flashed vividly behind my eyes. I heard the crack of bone when the rope dropped and felt the swinging toes skim the top of my head.

I cried for what was lost. What we all had lost. All different. All the same.

The sun was long gone when I started back to camp. But, at the last minute, I veered off toward the bridge. Just one more time.

I noticed a shift in energy when my boots hit the planks, almost like goosebumps on my skin, but not as innocuous. I wanted to see them. I needed to see them. I felt left behind, like they were free and living a life without me, only...I didn't think that made sense.

I walked slowly through to the other side of the bridge. The gloom settled deep into my bones, reassuring me that I had done the right thing by visiting the bridge one more time.

To my surprise, Amelia was waiting when I emerged, leaning against a large rock and holding a lantern.

"Hi," she said and gave a little wave.

"Hey." I gave my own wave, unhappy I had to redirect my thoughts. "What are you doing here?"

"Figured you were here. Did you see anything?"

"No." I couldn't tell her I felt them, but I also couldn't keep the sullenness from my voice at not seeing them.

"I did more research when I got back from the lake," she said. "I found only two, or two and a half, references about the ones hanging from the rafters."

"Really?"

She nodded. "Apparently, they're called, 'the hanging ladies.'" She air quoted. "One report said it was bunk. Another said the stories are purposefully hushed so not to drive off people from coming to the park. Parents don't want their kids seeing a bridge filled with suicide victims when they're on vacation. Or even the ghosts of suicide."

"I guess not," I said miserably. "But I want to know who they are."

"I think that'll be a hard dig. One of the posts kinda seemed conspiracy theory-ish, but they said the ones hanging were women who felt the pull of the jumper lady. That she calls out to depressed girls at their worst moments and forces them to hurt themselves. How messed up would it be if that was true? We feel bad for her, but she's calling girls to kill themselves all these years later?"

"Maybe she doesn't mean to do it," I said defensively. "Maybe it's not her calling, but her sorrow."

"If she keeps showing herself, then she means to, and that's bullshit," Amelia said. "The conspiracy poster said girls have been found hanging there as little as four years ago!"

"Amelia, these women, who were already isolated in pain, were then further isolated, and even forgotten, in death. And for what? Propriety and revenue?"

"The park has to make money, Piper. And I don't know I'd call it propriety just because parents don't want their kids to see something like that. Look how freaked-out you were, and still are."

"I'm fine," I snapped.

"Okay. Well…as cool as it was that you saw them, maybe we can put it aside and go back to camp." Amelia smiled cautiously when I didn't respond. "Unless…they're making you feel bad or like jumping or hurting yourself?"

"I didn't say that. I just think it's sad these women are forgotten."

"So do I. But if you're okay, then we should go back to camp and have a good time."

"It's so easy for everyone to have a good time." My anger swelled, attaching to anything that could feed it. "They can't have a good time. They're stuck here! Alone."

"I understand that, but unfortunately, Piper, there isn't anything we can do."

"Well, there should be! Because when something awful happens to you, like losing your baby when you planned nine months for it or when someone makes a decision that totally derails all the plans you had in life, it's quite frankly, fucked up."

"Piper..." Amelia reached out to me, speaking softly. "Are you okay?"

I quickly stepped back. When I realized I was crying, I put my hands over my face. The tears poured out. It was quiet, but unattractive and full of frustration.

"It's alright," she said, and she came close enough to hug me, but only put her hands on my arms. "Pain is just a phase, and it too shall pass."

"It's not going away," I sobbed.

"I thought you were doing really well."

"I am so stuck, Amelia. And then we get here, and he's right next to me, but he doesn't take my hand or even say good morning to me. It's exhausting waiting to be noticed by someone who's moved on."

"I'm so sorry, Piper. I guess, I knew you were a little sad. I had hoped...I don't know. Sometimes life takes us places we didn't want to go. And some things we didn't know we needed; we get."

"I didn't want what happened to me, Amelia. I was on a path, and he threw me off!"

"I know, but, certain change gives us trauma, and other change gives us healing or direction."

"For fuck's sake, Amelia! Stop talking to me like you're a self-help book!"

"I'm sorry," she said. "I don't know what to do! I don't know how to help you."

"Am I interrupting?"

Both Amelia and I startled.

"Noah?" I squinted, only making out his thin frame wearing our EMS uniform and his blond hair in the dark. "What are you doing here?"

"Why so angry? Can't I be here?"

"What? No," I said. "Why are you here?"

"You left a message, in the middle of the night, saying you saw a ghost jump off a bridge and other ghosts hanging from a ceiling, and then I didn't hear from you. Who does that?"

"So, you came all this way?"

"Yes," he said. "You sounded really upset."

"I was, but…no one really cares."

"Of course, I care. I'm here, aren't I?"

I opened my mouth, and for a moment nothing came out. "About these women, I meant. No one cared about them in life, why would they care in death?"

"They're ghosts, Piper."

"They were real people, Noah!"

"Okay, but what are we supposed to do?" When I didn't answer, he looked over at Amelia, who became obvious standing quietly to the side in the small lantern light. He nodded to her. "Hey, Am."

"Hey," she said.

We stood for a few moments. I think we were all trying to figure out if we were arguing and if we were, why?

"What are you going to do then?" Noah asked.

"About the ghosts?"

"Yes, Piper. About the ghosts."

"I don't know. She's a ghost, stuck in some torturous limbo. Forever jumping off the bridge to be with her stillborn baby because she doesn't know what else to do. And the others hung themselves because none of them knew how to get over what happened to them. And I get it! What's the fucking point? Move on to what?" I yelled, not understanding the intensity of my anger.

Amelia backed up.

"What is wrong with you?" Noah growled back at me. "You think everything is pointless and futile and awful when people are here for you, holding space, trying to make you laugh, trying to get you to notice—"

"Notice what?"

"I don't know. Anything!" Noah stepped back. "Notice something other than Erik and move on."

"Move on to what?" I asked again, hyperventilating. "I don't know what to do with myself. He was my boyfriend since I was seventeen."

"And now he's not," Noah said, forcing himself to be calm. "Piper, you can move past this."

"I don't know how!"

"Listen," said Amelia. "You're one of the most loyal people I know. I get it. But you don't have a choice. You move or you get stuck and end up...a ghost perpetually jumping or hanging from a bridge for eternity."

"I don't know how to…how to stop…" I wanted to say more. I wanted them to hear me. "I don't—"

"Come back Greta! Come back!" a man's panicked voice echoed.

"Shit." I looked around. "Who was that?"

"I just heard a screech," said Amelia.

"More like *what* was that?" said Noah, with his hands over his ears.

The dark sky opened up, and a brilliant full moon that should not be there, shone like a giant flashlight, bathing the bridge in the same ghostly silver-white glow as the first night I saw the ghosts. It was the old bridge with the open sides, not the covered bridge of this time, not the bridge of a moment ago.

"She's back," I said. "Look at the moon?"

"There's no moon," said Noah.

"Where is she?" whispered Amelia.

She came rushing from the narrow trail behind Noah. A ghostly glow with a heavy bundle of blankets clutched to her chest.

"Greta!" The man called, louder this time.

"Dammit," said Noah, and he put his hands over his ears. "That sound is just wrong."

The ghost woman, Greta, stopped next to him, and he stood very still. She turned her head, looking through him, then moved onto the bridge.

Amelia turned me to face her. "What's happening?"

"She's so heartbroken." I watched Greta sing to her baby. Agony tightened its grip around my heart. "It's not fair."

"Life isn't fair," whispered Amelia.

"She's in a loop of grief." Noah took my hand. "Tell her she can move on, Piper."

"Maybe..." I said. "Maybe some of us just can't do that."

With my words a half dozen or more eerie moon-glowing ghost girls stepped from the bushes around us. Some crying. Some holding rope. Some filled with rage. Some were dressed strangely old-fashioned or in rags. Some were crying into their phones, leaving messages before throwing the phone into the river. They walked back and forth, in and out of each other, weeping and yelling.

"It's freezing," said Amelia, her free hand rubbing the arm holding the lantern.

"It's trailing right up my back," Noah said.

To me, they felt warm, nurturing, like a friend calling.

The apparitions moved around us, onto the bridge and then back again. One went through me drenching me in her desperation, crippling my spirit with an ache that latched onto my insides. They needed me. They needed me with them. My torment had a home.

"Say something." I heard Noah say as if he were in another room. "Piper! Look at me!"

I blinked. He was in front of me now. He'd taken hold of my shoulders.

"Talk to me!"

"Get off me." I tried to wrench away from his grip. "You don't understand."

"Stop walking toward the bridge!"

"I wasn't!"

"You were," said Amelia. "We called, but you wouldn't listen."

"You were mumbling." Noah turned me away from the girls continuing their unending cycles—throwing ghostly ropes over the rafters, yelling into phones, Greta crying at the ledge. "Listen to me. It's okay to grieve. You just cannot live there forever."

It was hard to hear Noah's voice, the ghost-chatter was overwhelming. I put my hands over my ears. "I don't want to talk about it anymore!"

"I'm sorry, Piper. I'm sorry he ruined your life."

"He ruined ME!" The chaotic energy swirled, and I pulled against Noah's grip.

"He wasn't happy. But please, don't let his unhappiness ruin you."

"I gave all I had, Noah."

"And I am so sorry. But…I'm glad he left because he would have hurt you more if he'd stayed."

"You don't understand," I said. "You just can't say that and understand!"

The voices of the ghosts were a cacophony of sound calling to the bottomless black pit inside my chest, and I wanted to be back on the bridge.

"Piper!" He shook me, not hard, but enough. "Is this who you want to be? A shade of who you once were, reliving the night he broke up with you. Over and over. Ending up at the same bridge every night, throwing yourself into the river to live with the thing that died? Just a statistic in some ledger."

I flinched.

Noah's eyes widened. "Is that what you want to be, a forgotten statistic in some book somewhere. How would that make your sister feel?"

I felt something spark deep in my chest.

"All I'm doing is going through the motions. If I stop, it'll all be a memory, and I don't know how to come to terms with that."

"You have a choice now, Piper." Amelia hugged me. "You get to decide how you go into your future."

I looked at the ghosts around us. They could feel them, but I could see them. They needed me. They loved me. I opened my mouth, and Noah shook his head.

"Stop trying to figure out what you did wrong. Let's figure out what Piper needs to be happy."

"I don't know...I don't know how to stop trying!" I took a long stuttering breath. "I don't know how to stop trying to be better...for him," I said it, finally, and I felt mortified and defeated.

But the noise around me lowered. The ghosts shifted.

"I don't know how to say goodbye to him. And that makes me feel stupid and alone because he's said goodbye to me already."

The confession pushed at my emotional weight. The ghostly glow began to flicker. They coalesced on the bridge.

"You're not stupid, and you are not alone." Noah said. "You're hurt and trapped in your heartbreak, and that is nothing to be ashamed of."

"I can help you," said Amelia. "We can help, if you let us."

I cried; a burden of emotion began slowly pulling away from me. We were smooshed together. Amelia at my back and Noah in front supporting me. He wiped at my cheeks, such a small, kind gesture.

"You will not be a statistic," Noah said softly.

"I am not a statistic," I whispered.

The energy of Greta and her followers broke and then drifted farther away, broken-hearted that I wasn't going to follow them. And almost immediately their world became distant. The reality of what I had seen, what I had felt and what had just happened to me, began to fade, like an old memory or dream.

It was dark. I was shaking. The antiquated full moon was gone and with it the last of the apparitions. I took a few wavering breaths, feeling, strangely lucky, like I'd escaped something really fucking terrible.

"I thought I wanted to see the hangin' ladies," said Amelia. "I was wrong. I don't ever want to see what you saw."

Noah put his hand over my heart. "It's always going to take space here, but it will hurt less and less until you remember the good parts over the bad."

He said the words with such surety I wondered what he had endured in his life to give him the strength that fit him so comfortably. He knew I could get past this because he did, and he believed in me. They believed in me. And that helped me believe. They would not let me fall from the ledge.

"What do I do now?" I wiped at my face with my shirt sleeve.

"Do you want to be here?" asked Amelia.

"I want to go home," I said with surety.

"Then I will take you," said Noah.

"I won't look stupid?" I asked.

"No." Amelia laughed. "But who even cares?"

They both pulled me in for another hug, and I felt lighter than I had in over a year. How could I know that conceding to the pain would help me push past it? No one ever tells you that admitting you feel weak and vulnerable gives you strength.

"The truck's back there." Noah pointed over his shoulder. "Not even a quarter mile. We could just leave."

"You brought the ambulance?"

He shrugged. "I was in a hurry.

"No," I said. "I have to get my stuff. But will you both come with me and be there when I explain that I'm leaving?"

"Of course."

I looked at the bridge one last time before we started up the trail back to camp. I couldn't relate to Greta anymore. I pitied her, and I felt grateful, something I hadn't felt in a very long time.

What Sort of Woman

Cat Voleur

From down in the darkness, a baby cries.

The woman stumbles back from the edge onto the weather-worn planks of the old bridge and tries to catch her breath from the fall.

She wants to pretend nothing happened, to blame her imagination. Such a thing proves impossible with the cries still echoing into the night. They filter through the eerie void that surrounds her before finally fading into the abyss. At long last, the sound is contained only to her mind.

It's all in my head, she tells herself.

She stands from where she has fallen.

Another cry rings out.

This one is louder. More certain. Pervasive. It is a constant wail from below that demands attention.

Begs. Pleads. The sound calls out to that primal, maternal instinct that would not let a child suffer.

She begins to walk away.

The crying gets even louder with distance, and she pretends she doesn't hear.

What sort of woman are you? She asks, even as her pace quickens. *What sort of woman abandons a crying baby?*

Even before her car had broken down on the bridge, Madeline was having the worst day of her life.

It had been John's funeral today.

There had been complications.

All this last week her dreams have been filled with visions of the accident. The two of them had been fighting when it happened.

He'd been angry over something at work, and she'd been just as angry that he'd quit over it. Only that wasn't her problem at all. She'd actually been upset because she had good news for him, and he'd ruined it. He didn't want to celebrate. Barely two hours had passed of his unemployment and he was already so worried about money that he'd entirely forgotten their call at lunch, when he'd agreed to take her somewhere nice for dinner.

It feels utterly foolish now.

It had crushed her the night it happened. She'd been so frustrated. That was going to be the story they had about the day he found out, and she couldn't bear to tell such a sad story for the rest of their lives. So she'd started a fight instead of telling him what she had to say. Their voices were getting louder and louder as they talked over one another.

He looked over at her at just the wrong moment, angry, and the other car just came out of nowhere.

Now John would never know why going out had been so important to her that night, and she would never forget the anger in his eyes the last time he looked at her. He'd never hear her good news, and there was no longer good news to tell him if he were there.

Madeline doesn't know if it was the crash or the depressive episode triggered by his death, or the stress of funeral planning, or some other kind of divine punishment. All she knows is that she woke up bleeding, and now that last little piece of him is gone.

The part even he hadn't known about.

Madeline is as empty as a person can be.

She was too numb to cry as they had lowered the love of her life into the ground. She was too numb to register the stares and whispers her expressionless face had earned her from his friends and family. She is too numb, still, to try and help the baby.

There is no baby.

And she believes this. Almost.

People are cruel. That a newborn could be left alone under an old bridge, Madeline does not doubt. But that her car happened to break down at exactly the right place and time to hear it when it cried? On the exact day she learned she won't be a mother after all?

No.

She doesn't believe in such coincidences.

As she has felt pushed past the point of breaking all day, it seems far more feasible that her mind is starting to play tricks on her. It wants her to look back at what she's lost. It wants her to mourn what might have been.

There is no baby.

The cry might have been a figment of her imagination, but the girl is real.

She is lying in a pool of blood halfway between where Madeline stands and the first bend in the road toward the tree line.

Madeline's heart stops when the poor thing begins to move.

How is she still alive?

She rushes to kneel by the girl who stares up at her with wide, frightened eyes.

"It's you..." whispers the bloodied teenager before she erupts into weak coughs. Madeline doesn't need the light of her dying cellphone to see how dark the spittle is.

"Shhh," Madeline says in a way she hopes is calming. She digs out the device from her purse anyway, turning the back flashlight on to the girl. She wants to assess the damage of the wound beneath the tattered black dress.

It's not good.

"I…" whispers the girl. "I'm so…"

"It's okay," Madeline assures her. "You're okay. Save your strength."

But she persists.

"I'm…so…sorry."

●

Madeline would not have made it back to the car if the bridge were not close to where she had found the girl.

Too close.

Closer than should have been possible for how long she'd been walking on her own.

There are bigger things to worry about right now.

Her arms are burning from carrying the girl—who while toothpick thin, is nearly at a height with her. Now she's bleeding all over the passenger's seat of Madeline's car.

I made it worse. I shouldn't have moved her.

She ignores such thoughts. She had her reasons, and in any case, it's done now. All she can do is live with her decision. She digs around in the glove compartment for her first aid kit.

I don't think a bandage is going to do much.

She opens the box anyway and takes stock of the contents under the yellow glow of the overhead light.

The individually wrapped alcohol wipes are almost enough to break her into bitter laughter, but she prevails in her focus. She picks out the gauze, and the tiny pair of scissors.

First thing, she cuts away the soaking black fabric that still obscures the wound.

Wounds, she realizes. *There's more than one.*

There are three jagged lines opened in her flesh.

Claw marks?

She feels vindicated in her decision to bring her back now, certain there is something lurking in the dark. It's all she can do not to get distracted from her task by the thoughts of bears and wildcats.

Not daring to waste anymore time than she has to, she begins to wrap the gauze around the girl's stomach. There's enough to go around several times, but not enough to provide adequate pressure.

With the area as sterile as it's going to get, Madeline tears a strip free from around the ankles of the girl's long, ruined dress.

Only now does she realize how strange the attire is. The gown is made from a shiny, fake-satin costume fabric. What the girl was doing dressing up in summer, Madeline could not have said. She isn't even sure who or what the generic, Victorian ensemble is meant to represent.

It doesn't matter now.

She binds the wounds up as best she can while thinking about her next step.

They may have some shelter in the car, but she doesn't think the girl will last long enough for help to come. The car isn't working and her phone doesn't have service this far out in the middle of nowhere.

These were things she tried in the first place, reasons why she had been walking away from the bridge rather than waiting herself. Now she's not sure it's even safe to try and leave.

Her choices seem to be making a run for help, or staying and hoping for the best. Her luck hasn't exactly been good as of late.

Do I really want to watch the sun rise with a corpse in my car?

Her debate is cut short by the sound of a baby wailing from below the bridge.

She gives it more thought than she wants to.

With her headlights on, Madeline tries to peer out over the side of the bridge, to see if she can see the baby. Or a safe way down. Or anything at all.

Before, when she had checked, she'd estimated the drop down to the thin, rocky river to be about twenty or thirty feet.

Now she can't make out anything.

She's all too aware of how the cries grow softer as she looks for them, and louder every time she steps away. The sound is almost deafening by the time she decides to run.

I'm not abandoning the baby, she tells herself this time. *I'm going to bring back help.*

But this isn't entirely true.

She's terrified, and she wants to flee.

Only she can't.

No matter how long she jogs down the path, that first bend is always just out of reach. And every time she glances over her shoulder, she finds that she's just a few paces from the bridge.

This is always the same. It doesn't matter how fast or slow she travels, or how long she can resist checking her progress. The bridge is always just behind her and the baby's cries always echo.

There's no logical explanation to be had, and to Madeline's surprise, she finds she doesn't need one. Her brain is shutting down again, going silent.

Numb.

There is only so much a person can bear in a single day, and Madeline is well past her limit. She turns around and walks the twenty or so feet back to the car.

She sits beside her bloody passenger, defeated.

●

"You hear it too, don't you?"

Madeline looks over to the girl, surprised.

She thought the girl had lost too much blood to wake again without medical intervention. This is a sharp reminder that she's not a doctor.

"Hear what?" she asks.

"That...thing. It...it sounds like a baby?"

Madeline has gotten so used to the noise by this point that she's all but entirely drowned it out. The question draws her attention, though. She twists behind the steering wheel.

The girl looks pale and weak, but there is clarity in her eyes that had not been present when Madeline first found her.

"Why do you call it a thing?"

"I don't know what else to call it."

"But you don't think it's a baby?"

She shakes her head. "No…it attacked me."

The baby was the same thing that had attacked her?

"Tell me everything that happened."

"I came out here…I was going to scare my friends. But then I heard the crying. It didn't sound like a ghost…it sounded real…"

"A ghost?"

She nods.

"What do you mean a ghost?"

It's you, the girl had said before she had apologized in her gaudy black dress.

"We're on The Crybaby Bridge."

Madeline's head starts swimming at the new information. Ghosts. Scares. Friends. An urban legend from her childhood that she only half remembers. The details of her situation threaten to pull her under the tide of madness, but the girl speaks again.

"It wasn't a baby…or a ghost." Her voice is cracked and thick from the misery of her injuries.

"Can you tell me what it was?"

The girl shakes her head.

Another dead end.

But then she speaks. "It was like the shadows were moving."

Madeline thinks back to the darkness she'd seen under the bridge, the massive ocean of ink that was waiting just below them.

"We have to get out of here," she says.

"Wait," whispers the girl.

"We don't have—"

"Wait." The girl insists, her voice low, but strong.

Madeline waits in complete silence.

She waits a full minute before it dawns on her.

The crying has stopped.

"We need to move. Now."

The sound has stopped trying to lure them closer, which can only mean one thing.

It's too late to share her revelation.

Glass shatters.

Steel screeches.

It is the accident all over again, as the creature comes to them.

Three high school kids approach the infamous bridge just before midnight. It was a longer hike than any of them anticipated.

Owen is sounding winded.

None of them have spoken much the last ten or fifteen minutes up the road.

Liam slides his phone from his pocket to check the time.

11:53.

There should still be enough time to get there before the woman jumps, but there won't be enough time to set up the frame and still record the intro in that same spot.

"Blake, you ready to record?"

"Sure, give me a sec."

They slow down for Blake to adjust their backpack.

"What the hell is that?" Owen asks.

Liam turns around to look at the clunky camera Blake is fiddling with.

"Yeah, what the hell?"

"Haven't either of you two ever seen a camcorder?"

Neither of them have, but that's beside the point.

"Why aren't you just recording on your phone?" Liam asks.

"Ghosts don't show up on phones, idiot."

They say this as if it's common knowledge everyone should have.

"We're going to miss it," Owen says.

"I'm almost ready."

Liam doesn't feel as sure about their set-up anymore, but he doesn't want to lose the illusion of control he's been building up all night. "All right. We'll record the intro when you're ready. Owen, take your phone out just in case."

"Got it," Blake insists. They roll their eyes when Liam pauses for Owen to get the camera up on his phone.

"Got it," he confirms.

Liam takes a breath and looks into both cameras. "Tonight we are going to Ohio's most haunted location," he says. "Crybaby Bridge. The time is…" He checks his phone and it's all he can do not to swear. "Eleven fifty-five pm, which means we should be just in time to catch the ghost."

He starts walking again, faster than before. Blake keeps up easily despite the bulky camera, but Liam is sure the only audio Owen is going to capture will be that of his own huffing and panting.

We should have left sooner.

Blake, ever the pro, hops in with a question. "For our non-local viewers, do you want to tell us about the bridge?"

He must have practiced this part about a dozen times, though never while jogging through the woods. "They say the bridge is where an unwed mother threw herself into the water after being scorned by the father of her child and disowned by her family. She drowned in the river, leaving the baby to die all alone. They say if you cross the bridge at exactly midnight, you can see her ghost jump again." He looks over his shoulder for dramatic emphasis. "They say you can hear the death cries of the child to this day."

Owen screams and drops his phone, the woods suddenly growing that much darker.

Liam whips his head back around and freezes to the spot.

He would scream too, if he could.

An older woman in a torn, lace dress is limping down the path toward them. It's a more modern cut than he would have guessed, but black as the legends say: well-suited to wear to her own, watery grave.

He staggers off the path, out of her way when she draws close enough for the group to see her hands and legs are both streaked with red.

Blake is the last one to step back, filming still. "Hello?"

Shut up, he wants to tell them.

Everyone knows not to talk to a ghost.

The woman slows but does not stop walking.

"Can we help you?" They try again.

"You can help my baby," she whispers. "My baby needs to be fed."

Just like that she walks around the bend and disappears from view.

As if on cue, a baby cries in the distance.

It is nearly dawn when Madeline breaks through the tree line and out into the real world.

She could pretend for her own sanity that the sun broke whatever magic had kept her captive near that bridge, but she's a little past the point of sugarcoating her own actions.

She paid for her freedom in the blood of the dead girl's friends.

It had let her go when she had sent the others its way, and Madeline is too numb to feel bad about it now. Either she has succumbed to her delusions, or it was real, and she has narrowly avoided her exact vision of Hell.

It wouldn't matter, she tells herself.

And she believes it. Almost.

They wouldn't have listened to me even if I had told them the truth.

She'll never know for sure, but she thinks she's right. A warning isn't so different than a local legend, or the sound of a baby crying. It's something that good people will investigate.

But it's something Madeline survived.

Time and the Bear

Derek Heath

Spangles of sunlight dappled the water, shallow crests foaming in the swelling shadow of a long, narrow bridge high above. Long sheer cliffs thrust out of the muddy edges of the river; at either end of the bridge, a wide scar of reddish earth was ruined by an explosion of treeline, thick green pine and aspen trunks swaying softly in the breeze.

A shape emerged from the eastern bank of trees. Chunks of stone crunching beneath rugged walking boots. As if surprised to have escaped the cloying dark of the forest, the shape stopped, looked out upon the bridge and closed its eyes in an expression that looked like relief.

Anders had made it.

Fingers tucked into the tight straps of a bulky, thirty-kilogram backpack, he swayed for a moment and breathed deeply, the cool wind caressing the thick, striated mess of an orange beard that, over many days, had covered his jaws and neck. His hair was long and tangled, his shirt stained green and black with soil. Sweat pooled in his armpits and between his legs, trickling down his back.

Reaching up to run a hand through his hair, Anders opened his eyes and took a cautious step toward the bridge. It must have been a good thousand yards long, wooden slats knitted to a framework of rope and twine that bowed in the middle, a great thin hammock of planks and netting that jounced even before he'd laid a foot upon it.

Standing right at the end of the bridge, Anders looked down into the softly-churning waters below and smiled. The air was cool and pleasant, the light of the slowly-waning sun a miasma of beautiful gold and pink. He was nearly home; the thought alone of sinking into a thick, foam mattress was incredible.

Drawing in a deep breath, Anders finally stepped onto the bridge.

A gargantuan weight barreled into his back, vice-like jaws clamping down around his skull and puncturing the bone and cartilage of his neck. There was no time to scream. Before he could react at all his head was ripped from his body in a savage spray of red and pink, and all he could see was a yellowed, serrated set of teeth—then nothing—

I

—and then he emerged from the trees.

After a second that seemed to last an eternity, Anders blinked. He was standing where he had been only moments before, looking out onto the bridge. A few steps back, perhaps. Frozen stiff, he tried to blink away a smattering of black needlepoints in his vision. Shook his head.

Slowly, he reached up to feel his neck.

Was he dreaming?

The flesh felt real against the pads of his fingers, the bone beneath solid and intact.

But he still felt the sensation of enormously powerful jaws closing around his throat, ripping major arteries in a gushing explosion of hot, wet pain, tearing his head from his body…

He hadn't drunk a drop of alcohol in days, had only partaken of small and disappointing rations of marijuana since leaving the trail. Not enough to hallucinate, and certainly not after a few hours. Perhaps it was lack of sleep or food. Perhaps the sensation was just that: a sensation. Stepping up to the bridge, he looked down into the water and frowned. The water sparkled in exactly the same way it had seconds ago.

Slowly, he turned.

And the bear smashed out of the trees in a streak of brown and black, its face ripped open in the center where a great bony maw of teeth and thick, black tongue yawed into an enraged cavern. Thick, gnarled claws punched into Anders' chest, and he stumbled backward onto the bridge, barely landing on his back before the bear twisted its head and closed its enormous jaws around his neck. Anders screamed, a spray of thick hot blood exploding out of his mouth as his spinal column was twisted open.

Pain.

And then—

2

—and then he emerged from the trees.

Anders staggered forward, his entire body shuddering as an overwhelming cloak of terror swaddled him, tightening around his throat. Both hands went to his neck, and he felt desperately for any bite-marks, anything at all, but there was nothing. He was standing a little way back from the bridge, right where he'd been before...

Panicking suddenly, Anders turned around, gazing back into the trees. "What the hell is going on?" he whispered. The treeline was still, the only sounds the frantic pounding of his heart and the tinny rattling of batteries in his digital wristwatch as he raised his hands to run them through his hair.

His eyes flitted left and right, scanning the trees for movement. Nothing. Nothing there at all. Why would there be? There was no bear.

There was no bear.

Anders laid a hand across his chest, drawing deep breaths to try and slow his heartbeat.

No bear.

He'd imagined it. A brief spell of exhaustion-induced hallucination, that was all. And it was over now.

This time he heard it before he saw it, his ears attuned to the silence so that the splintering *crunch* of wood immediately drew his attention to the shadow barrelling out of the trees. But even then, it was too late. Before he could take a single step back, he was screaming into the bear's mouth as a hot, wet cavern of teeth and tongue crushed his skull into the pulp of his brain.

3

And then he emerged from the trees.

Anders doubled over as bile punched up his throat, an acid bath pouring out of his mouth as a dirty red rattail and spilling onto his boots. His wet sputtering turned to an agonised howl, and he screamed into the earth, hands clamped over his ears. A distant clump of trees shook as a murmuration of fluttering black shapes erupted from its boughs, shocked from their roost by the deafening outpouring of confusion.

Neck sore from some non-existent, phantom pain, Anders wheeled around to face the trees. His gaze immediately settled on the spot in the treeline from where the bear had come.

Two tiny points of white light, so insignificant it was no wonder he hadn't seen them before, stared back at him from the dark between the trees.

A flash of hungry teeth.

"What the fuck," Anders breathed, then a titanic clawed paw smashed into one of the trees, and the bear launched itself forward, black lips peeling back, the tiny points of its eyes becoming yellow pools of rage as they caught the sunlight.

Anders' eyes widened as he realised he knew what was coming next. He staggered back and to the side, breaking free of the stunned shell that had encased him and taking a single step out of the reach of the bear's swinging, slack jaws—

With a sickening *crack* the vice of the bear's maw burrowed into his shoulder, immediately dislocating his left arm and punching his ribs into his back. Anders' eyes bulged, and he screamed in agony. Somewhere at the back of his skull, a subconscious, flaring red part of his mind was momentarily relieved that at least the bear hadn't ripped his head off his neck this time. Then the bear ripped a chunk out of his shoulder and roared, an enormous broad shape looming over him and bellowing hot spittle and meat into his face.

It clapped, punching its paws into his skull and puncturing his brain instantly.

Everything went black.

4

Anders stumbled out of the trees and kept stumbling, head swimming, thick bolts of pain like lightning across his shoulder and chest. Glancing quickly back into the trees, he staggered forward and lurched onto the bridge, suddenly aware that even if he couldn't stop the bear from coming, he could at least run from it.

Surely it wouldn't follow him onto the bridge. It was an animal—a huge animal, but nonetheless one that was sure to be just a little reluctant of throwing itself onto a narrow funnel of wood and string—and it was these thoughts that propelled Anders forward, slamming his heel onto the bridge and instantly rolling his ankle.

"Fuu—uuuck!" he yelled, tumbling onto his front on the bridge. It swung madly as his weight crashed into the slats, and as he reached out to grab the nearest rope support, it swayed and bent with the movement.

A colossal weight slammed into his back, and he screamed as bony claws pierced his flank and shoulder.

"Fuuuuu—"

The bear swung its jaws down and ripped a chunk of meat from his neck, slopping meat hungrily down its throat and punching Anders' convulsing body into the wood.

9

Anders stepped breathlessly out of the trees and staggered forward, not risking a look back, keeping his eyes on the ground as he lunged onto the bridge and heaved his body into a run.

Phantom pains erupted all over his body—echoes, memories of teeth and claws and broken bones—as the bridge bowed beneath his thumping feet. The backpack swung heavily on his back, the clattering of steel pots muffled through layers of clothing and waterproof material. His vision was foggy. He kept his eyes on the edge of the bridge, a good kilometer-plus away—a thousand yards, now—nine-hundred-ninety-five—

He wasn't fast enough.

The bear ploughed into him and Anders yowled as sharp knives raked his back, spraying the wood with blood. Warmth gushed down his spine as he tumbled into the rope supports, his neck snapping immediately as his skull caught in the netting and twisted.

15

Anders crumpled, stumbling out of the woods and crashing into the reddish dirt, his knees buckling beneath him as his whole body exploded with fatigue. When he had finished vomiting he tipped his head back and screamed.

The sound was enough to shake enormous clots of birds from the trees. He yelled until his throat was coarse as sandpaper, and his voice cracked and died in his mouth, and then he sobbed into his hands, his face stinging and hot, his lungs burning.

"Why," he moaned, his voice barely a whisper.

The answer came in the form of a low, rumbling bellow behind him.

Anders wept, and as he cradled his skull in his hands the bear lurched up and loomed over his body and struck, plunging its claws into his neck.

24

It felt like half an hour had passed. But the sun still hung exactly where it had been before the bear; the clouds, what thin wisps of them stained the ichor of the sky, had not moved either. Far below him the same swell of water gushed beneath the bridge.

He stood at the edge of the woods for a good thirty seconds, just watching the sky.

Was this all there was? All there was going to be?

Anders had a sudden thought. Raising his wristwatch, he fumbled with the controls for a moment, a tiny beep accompanying every jab of a button. Satisfied that the settings were correct, he started the timer and watched.

One second.

Two seconds.

Three—

The shadow of the bear thrust out of the woods behind him and before Anders could count to four, his body was ripped in half in a warm spurt of blood and gore. Moments after he had died, parts of him began to plop into the water far below.

25

Quicker this time.

The second he stepped out of the woods, Ander looked at his wristwatch. Set the timer with a trembling hand and watched the display as the seconds snicked past. *One. Two. Three.*

Twelve.

Twenty.

Thirty-five.

He drew in a breath and held it, suddenly acutely aware of the presence behind him in the trees. He could sense it breathing on the air, feel its eyes boring into the back of his skull.

Forty-two.

The tiny *crack* of a dead branch as the bear took its first step forward.

Fifty.

Anders lowered the watch and counted in his head.

Seconds passed. A few of them, at least.

Then the left side of his skull smashed into the right and teeth the size of his thumbs splintered his jawbone in two.

32

He had timed it a few times now, and it seemed apparent that he had about a minute—somewhere between fifty-five and fifty-nine seconds, anyway— from the moment he stepped out of the woods to the very second the bear crushed his skull in.

What could he do in a minute?

He could run. He had tried a few times to make it across the bridge, but he never got far enough.

Well, run faster.

He could jump. Would the bear follow him over the cliff and into the river? Could he *make* a jump like that? If something *other* than the bear killed him, would the circadian loop he'd found himself in continue? Or would he just…die?

And what had caused all this? Was it the bear?

Was it him, somehow?

Or something else?

"Think," he whispered. "What can you do in sixty seco—"

His eyes bulged out of his head as his brain was ripped from his nervous system.

40

So, running wasn't an option.

There was no way he could make it across the bridge. At his best calculation—and this was only approximate, for he could only use his own exhausted judgement to gauge the length of the bridge—the gap between the cliffs was about a thousand yards. Maybe a few more. Call it a thousand, to be safe.

He remembered that Usain Bolt had run something like forty-five kilometers an hour at his highest, which amounted to around seven hundred and forty-five meters per minute. Mentally, he calculated that to be about eight hundred and ten yards. Eight-fifteen, maybe.

So, if he could run at Usain Bolt speed, he'd make it eighty percent of the way across the bridge. Nearly the whole length.

But Anders wasn't Usain Bolt. And so far, he had only been able to make it about one-fifth of the distance.

So what? You don't have to make it across the bridge.
You just have to outrun—
—the bear ploughed into him.

45

Anders launched straight into a sprint, lurching for the bridge at what he considered to be breakneck pace, even if it wasn't Bolt-speed.

He made it a good three hundred yards before the bear caught up to him, closing the distance in four or five long, loping strides and knocking into his spine. The bridge swayed side-to-side as they tumbled over each other in a rampage of brown-black fur and shredded skin. He knew the bear's face well by now. He looked into its eyes in that last moment, a glaring, hungry yellow.

The color of death.

80

Something different.

Anders glanced at the sun—still there, hanging right on the horizon where it had been all this time, though he felt he'd been doing this for a good hour now. Then he turned around and ran back into the trees.

Forget the bridge.

He burst through a hanging network of vines and tumbled downhill, boots punching into the soft earth as dead things crackled and shifted around him. Trees flashed past as he raced through the undergrowth, ignoring the scratching and clawing of thick knee-high thorns and branches.

He'd been running for what felt like an hour when he cursed himself for not trying this before. Of course. It was the fucking bridge, that was when the loop had started—he just had to get out of range of it before the end of his minute, *that* was how he'd escape this nightmare—why had he never tried running back into the woods?

Anders tore to the right and ducked a low-hanging branch. This is it, he thought frantically, this is my escape. Keep running, don't look back, don't think about it.

He didn't have time to think about it.

His whole body smashed into the moss-covered trunk of a thick aspen, and he collapsed, tipping backward—straight into the arms of the titanic bear that had followed him from the treeline.

A minute had passed. Blood spattered his wristwatch.

123

How do you deal with a bear attack?

As far as Anders recalled, it was one of two things. Either you stood as tall as possible and tried to intimidate the bear—make as if to fight it, if necessary—or you cowered, showed submission, let it know *you* know who's in charge.

There was no third option.

There was no *run*.

He had been going about this entirely wrong. He had to turn round, look the bear dead in the eyes, face it head-on.

Anders turned. Looked in the direction of the watching bear. Decided upon option one, and stood as straight as he could muster. This had to be it.

And if not, you'll have the chance to try again.

The bear lumbered out of the woods.

Anders' body tightened, and he growled, narrowing his eyes.

It was a grizzly. He had known this for some time now, though classifying the animal hadn't been high on his list of priorities. He remembered every time the bear had slaughtered him, still felt every agonizing, shredding pain; there wasn't an inch of his body that hadn't been torn or pulped or punctured.

Anger enveloped him suddenly, and he roared, lunging toward the bear with his hands flexed into knotted, white-knuckled hooks. "Come on, then!" he yelled. "Come fucking fight me, if you think you're hard enough!"

Option one wasn't it.

The bear smashed its whole weight into him, and Anders toppled onto his rucksack in the dirt, thick claws punching into his gut and ripping out coil after coil of intestine as he twitched and gargled.

124

Option two, then.

Anger still pumping through him, mania immediately filling his veins, Anders turned and slung off the backpack. It landed with a rattling *thwump* in the dust.

Eyes locked on the bear, Anders lowered his head in submission and dropped to his knees.

Be small. Don't let it think you want to fight.

Briefly he wondered if the grizzly could remember all of this, too. What if this mad, repeating minute wasn't localized to him? What if it was the whole world? Everybody had been living out the same minute for the past two hours, again and again, and they would forever…it was a glitch in the system, something had suddenly and fundamentally broken in the universe, and time was ruined.

Or maybe it was just him and the bear. Locked together in this moment because…well, because someone up there hated them both.

Maybe if he died enough times, whatever mad god was doing this would be satisfied and take time off pause.

No, that couldn't be it. Curling his head into his chest, he breathed slowly and listened to the bear's padding footsteps. It had to be survival. That was his only way out. Survive this minute, and his life would continue as it had meant to.

And this was how he survived. By treating the bear as a superior, by showing it he meant no harm. *This* was—

125

Anders closed his eyes and stifled screams.

The bear came for him after fifty-nine seconds, as it always did.

He began again.

159

And began again.

180

And again.

246

Again.

500

Again.

2,789

Anders tumbled forward, scrambling for the cliff edge. He didn't care if plummeting into the river killed him for real. Ended him.

He just wanted this to stop.

He rolled over the edge and, for a second, he was flying, then that second seemed to stretch into an eternity, wind whistling past his ears, the long stripe of the bridge above him shrinking, growing narrower as his arms flailed uncontrollably, and he rolled over himself, again, again, crashing down toward the water below.

His head smashed into the cliff edge, and he bounced. Left foot jolted into his knee, bone shearing flesh, as a boulder punched upward. Water surface smacked him hard.

He floated, stars swimming in his vision, blood pooling into the river around him and turning to thick clots of red mist. The water was unbelievably cold, immediately freezing his veins. He gazed up, into the sky, musing upon the permanence of death. That was how it should be.

Or maybe this was hell. Maybe he was doomed to repeat his last minute on Earth because whoever ruled this nightmarish afterlife had decided that was man's worst punishment.

He could have sworn a good eighty seconds had passed when the grizzly bear appeared at the cliff edge high above him, poking its face into his line of sight and growling down at the river.

Its ears twitched. And he saw something else, too: clinging to the bottom of the bridge, something small and worm-like and pale. As he stared blankly up at the putrid-looking thing, it wriggled. What the hell was that?

Then the grizzly leapt, ploughing off the cliff with all the grace and savagery of a bird of prey, and as it smashed into him and punched him underwater, and he screamed with a mouthful of icy, wet silt and blood, he thought:

At least it was different this time.

5,012

Anders staggered out of the trees and fell onto his face, where he lay in the dirt and waited for death.

He had tried everything he could think of. When these attempts had failed, hundreds of times each, he had tried them all again. And again. And again.

He went through periods of depression where he didn't bother at all, just crumpled in the sand and let it happen to him. Then, when even this grew tiring, he seemed to build up an urge to try again, to refuse defeat and try something else. Or, more accurately, something he had already tried more often than he could count. The bear couldn't be outrun, or fought— he had spent hours upon hours of repeated minutes digging items out of his backpack to use as a weapon, and each had been unsuccessful—and it couldn't be submitted to, dominated, tricked.

After he had tried a few more things, he fell into his depression again.

A cycle within a cycle.

Even when he drowned—smashed his face on a tree—stumbled into a wild dog's den in the woods—

got bitten by a snake—the loop restarted. Didn't matter if the bear killed him, or the fall, or if—as he had begun to do, just lately—he found a way to kill himself.

It never ended.

Was it a lesson?

"Doesn't matter," he murmured into the dirt. "Bear's coming."

The padding footsteps loudened, and he closed his eyes.

31,780

All his agony was mental.

His body reset, just like everything else, at the beginning of every minute. He was only as tired, as hungry, as thirsty as he had been at the start of it all.

But he hadn't eaten or drunk anything in what felt like a month, and he hadn't slept. His body was completely unwounded, but he had suffered every imaginable injury and death over and over, one after the other in an unrelenting, exhausting pattern.

Mentally, there was nothing left of him. Every time he emerged from the treeline he was weaker, lesser, closer and closer to real, permanent death. But it was like approaching an asymptote: it didn't matter how he *felt*, because physically, he was fine.

Until the bear came.

Again, just like before, it did.

90,505

This time he walked right into its arms, almost begging it through tears to just get it over with, kill him already.

It seemed to relish the kill more this time, playing with him, ripping softly, tearing chunks from his face and stomach with its teeth, almost nuzzling him.

It did this for about a minute, then it severed his carotid, and he flopped limply into its mouth.

420,686

A fever dream.

He woke, hot and dazed, and the bear was above him, but further away than before. Then he was sinking into the Tartarus of its mouth, sinking, sinking...

Flies buzzed around the open door of the cabana, and the ocean outside swelled softly. Food poisoning. The shrimp. He threw up again.

Claws plunged into his stomach, and his cheek grazed the dirt.

851,000

Anders remembered something. Something he had seen...months ago? Weeks? Days?

About a minute ago, he supposed.

Something pale and worm-like, suckered to the bottom of the bridge.

"Huh," he said, stumbling forward a step. Maybe he should look for—

1,904,371

Anders lunged forward, shucking the backpack from his shoulders and scrambling onto the bridge. The nineteenth plank, he remembered. That was the weakest. Thundering forward, he counted—*three, eight, fourteen*—

Nineteen.

Dropping to his knees, he fumbled desperately with the plank. He had done this so many times now that he knew just how to pull, just how to lever the wretched thing so that it ripped loose from the bracing rope on the left within a few seconds. Then all he had to do was catch the damn thing before it—

The slat tore away in his hands, exposing a sliver of nothing in the bridge through which he saw the river below.

Something pinkish and gelatinous slithered away from him, a wet sucking sound accompanying the slug-like movement of the thing beneath the bridge.

"Fuck you!" Anders yelled, thrusting his arm through the gap and fumbling about beneath the bridge. He slapped something warm and wet, felt it squirm as he grabbed frantically for it. His fingers clutched it, and he heaved back, cringing at the putrid smell and the feeling of warm, meaty slime in his hand. "Come here, you bastard!"

Claws in his back. His grip loosened, and he fell forward, succumbing instantly to the jaws that clamped over his neck and ripped his head off his body.

2,000,192

Lunge forward. Lose the backpack.

Bridge. Nineteenth plank. He'd tried the rest, not loose enough. Or too far away.

Drop. Grab. Wrestle—

The plank came loose, and he jammed both arms down through the hole. Grabbed, swiping at thin air until—

Practically hugging the thing, he heaved with all his strength and squeezed its wriggling, hissing body up between the slats and onto the bridge.

It lashed out with a stubby, segmented tail, its piercing cry one of irritation, not pain. And then it writhed out of his hands, slopping onto the bridge in a blur of pink and white and rolled away, plummeting off the side of the bridge and toward the water, leaving him empty-handed.

"NO!" he screamed, scrambling to the edge of the bridge. "NOT AGAIN! PLEASE!"

The bear came.

2,304,332

Forward. Backpack. Bridge.

Nineteen.

Pull. Grab.

Lumbering footsteps behind him as he slammed the worm-thing's wriggling body onto the bridge and pinned it.

"What the fuck is going on?!" he yelled into its face. It squirmed, its face nothing more than a ring of teeth in a shallow black pit. It squawked as he slammed his knee into its segmented midsection. It was the size of a pillow, a little longer maybe, with barbs and bumps beneath its membrane-coated skin. "Tell me! What the fuck is—"

Bear.

2,558,701

Nineteen.

Grab.

"What's happening to me?" Anders screamed, slamming the worm into the wooden slats of the bridge.

It hissed, its round maw yawing open, hooked barbs shooting out from within like thin, black tongues.

"*ANSWER ME!*"

Bear.

4,068,942

The worm screeched. Anders shook it, begging through tears.

"Answer me, answer me! Please, just fucking answer me, please!"

Bear.

19,540,328

"PLEASE, FOR THE FUCKING LOVE OF GOD, ANSWER ME!"

Bear.

384,701,888

Bear.

700,382,901

"Please—"

"Fine!" the worm shrieked, its voice strangled and unnatural. "Fine, just...just stop! Jesus!"

Stunned, Anders's grip loosened, and he recoiled. Blinked.

It wasn't real. Couldn't be. He was hallucinating.

He'd finally—after ten, fifteen, twenty, *however many* years of this—gone completely, irrecoverably mad.

"Make it stop," he whispered.

III

"*Fine,*" the mucus-covered creature hissed.

When Anders looked over his shoulder, there was no bear.

Then, to his horror, it lumbered out of the trees. An enormous, shadowy shape, its face locked in a tight, knotted mask of hunger and unadulterated predatory rage. Its claws hung by its sides, huge and glinting in the fading sunlight.

It stood at the end of the bridge and watched him.

"What the hell is this?" Anders breathed. "Why isn't it coming?"

Before the worm-creature could answer, the bear exploded.

Anders screamed as the grizzly detonated into a visceral slop of blood and bone, furry hunks of flesh spattering the bridge as more rained into the river and streaked the cliff with red. "What the fuck?!"

He turned back to the worm.

"What are you? Start fucking talking, now!"

The worm spoke, and its voice was like the shrieking of a faraway baby. Its whole body rippled and wobbled as its jaws moved. "I am time," it said.

"What the fuck does that mean?"

"I have been here for a long time," it whispered. "I *am* time. Do you know the things I can do?"

"I've been fermenting a few theories," Anders said gruffly. "Why are you doing this to me?"

For a second that seemed to last a lifetime, the worm looked up at him with its awful, eyeless face. Finally, it giggled. "I've been...playing."

Anders fumed.

"I used to be like you, you know. Then I discovered myself. I can't die. Can't age. But as time moved around me—backwards, forwards, round and round in circles—I changed. Became…god. God of time. Time itself. Do you know what happens to a creature who lives for millions of eternities, caught in time, straddled by it…broken by it? A creature who has seen time move in every conceivable direction and been unchanged by it, even as its mind attunes to the endless?

"I.

"*Am.*

"Time."

Anders shook his head. "And what do you want with me?"

The worm grinned, hook-like teeth shivering in its gummy, circular mouth. "Just a few more minutes."

"No," Anders started, his eyes going wide. "No, you can't—"

A shadow fell over him, and he looked up.

The bear roared and a hot, wet darkness swallowed him.

1,945,382,304

Anders was dizzy. Ever-dying. Never-dying. He sobbed endlessly, screamed into the mouth of the beast that chased him onto the bridge, again and again and againandagainandagainagainagain…

Time stretched and snapped around him. He had spent lifetimes in this minute, dozens of lifetimes. He was unchanged. And yet…

Bear.

136,890,473,190,192

The bridge was a sloppy, feverish blur in the landscape. The bear was coming. Time was endless. He was endless.

When he looked down, vision fading, madness seeping through his brain, he could swear that his arms had begun to shrink.

936,473,201,495,382,493,001

Time could contain him no longer. He could feel the worm's control of this endless relentless universe fading, feel his body slipping between moments, his features less defined, his limbs conjoining as cell growth and repair—all bodily functions—stopped, ceased, shut down by his irreparably declining mental state, but forced into shape by his body, emerging from the trees again and again, each time smashed into a different configuration by the bear—

He had stopped feeling it. A long time ago, longer than he knew, he had stopped feeling pain.

Feeling anything.

He had forgotten his name. But that was *millennia* ago.

47,384,302,493,105,684,302,503,593

His legs no longer worked. He was no longer sure he had any. He slithered forward, time pulling at him, his expanding mind pulling back. Unable to die, unable to grow, but permanently learning, attuning, becoming…

His body was suckered to the bridge. Almost entirely blind, he scanned the dark haze of the treeline for a shape. A lumbering, clawed shape thundering toward him.

Something split open. He couldn't tell if it was something inside him or all around him, if the world had opened or his mind had finally shattered.

A shape emerged from the trees.

A memory, faint as anything.

He thought the shape might be called *Anders*.

The creature on the bridge trilled excitedly.

If he had an eternity to kill—and it had been evident, many thousands and millions of lifetimes ago, that he did—then he might as well start having some fun.

On Patrol At Copperhead Bridge

Ray Daley

Welcome to Copperhead Bridge.

The red plank surrounds had bleached under decades of the summer sun. Pitch pine and oak, with a cast iron subframe and superstructure. Go ahead and ignore the signs hanging at each end which say it was built in 1835 by William Henry Thompson as a gift to the local people. Don't waste your time looking up that legendary benefactor either. *He doesn't exist and never did.*

Here's the truth of the matter, as known by any local over the age of forty. The whole bridge was built in a little under four weeks, across the shortest point of the Ottumwa River, here in Rochester Parish, Louisiana. During February 1983, for a movie. *Across The River Of Tears*, starring Richard Thomas. Yes,

John-Boy Walton to those old enough to remember him as such.

Which, ironically, never got released. It's still sitting in some studio archive, somewhere, long forgotten now.

Various carpenters, sheet metal workers, welders, painters and finishers were seconded from Industrial Light and Magic.

Sure, you'll hear the odd fairytale, how it was named after the snakes which abound in these parts. Or you could do your research like we did, and discover the only copperhead snake was being kept in a wildlife exhibit by a certified herpetologist, just outside Baton Rouge.

We were here before the bridge, and we'll be here long after it falls into the Ottumwa River too.

I'm Corporal Mason Manoit, and this is Senior Agent Lisa Francis. This is our beat. We patrol over, and around the Copperhead Bridge wildlife management area, the WMA for short. It is quite a mouthful, after all.

Our job here is to ensure no non-indigenous game species are being taken across state lines without the correct paperwork. We'll occasionally offer support to local law enforcement officers, as well as on-scene paramedic backup. Heck, you need us for anything, just holler.

Oh. You might need to shout louder. *Or bring a Ouija board.*

No. It's not a joke. *Death never is.*

●

April 1983

The cameras had only stopped rolling a week ago, but the movie folks had made an agreement to build a structure strong enough to stay here. You can always spot a local. Those who knew the real story behind the bridge. I'd even caught a couple of crooks from out of state, pretending to be locals. Yeah, locals are easy to notice. Unless your mind is on other things. Dad had passed less than a month ago, a bad stroke which took him out in under an hour, according to the coroner. That memory was still burning a hole in my heart. And my brain too, it seemed. "Afternoon, Game Warden. Need to check your vehicle for any livestock, please?"

He was eighty if he was a day. You could have hidden a mess of billy-goats in that beard, too. "Sure, I've popped the trunk, officer. Got five lake trout in a cooler. Paperwork is taped around the handle, as per your instructions."

He meant the fishery guidelines. Then I caught his name on the license he'd handed me. Yeah, I knew him. Well, I'd known his son. Served alongside him for a few months. "Oh, Andy. It's you. Sorry, dude, did you get a new truck? I wouldn't have stopped you if I'd recognized it. You're always in compliance, man. One of the good guys."

Andy laughed. "You know me too well, Mason. My son was a warden before he passed away. Never did get to thank you two for coming to the service. You're more than welcome to one of those trout in case you're fixing to fry later tonight?"

He knew full well I couldn't take a gift on the job. Then I noticed something wasn't quite right. His eyes flicked constantly to the back seat. He wasn't alone? "Listen, Andy. I've kept you tied up more than long enough today, you go on home." I passed back the license, mouthing "Back seat? Thumbs up, if not."

Andy just shook his head. "I'm tired. I'll see you next week, Mason. Say thanks to Lisa for me, okay?"

As Andy's pick-up pulled away, I was already on the radio. "Fish and Game twelve to unit fourteen. Stop that Ford before the state line. Ask the driver to step out for a sobriety check. FYI, it's actually a ten thirty-one. Back-seat. Over."

"Unit fourteen here. Understood, Mason. Out."

We weren't merely wildlife officers. Under federal law, we also had discretionary police powers. To stop, search, and arrest if need be. The handcuffs and guns weren't merely for show. We had already helped local PD enforce more than a dozen warrants in the parish over the last three months. Some folks thought we'd be much too busy providing security to these movie people, keeping looky-lou's away from the cameras. Only they had brought their own security with them. So we were more than able to protect and serve.

Don't quibble. It might not say that on the side of our truck, but we keep the people safe and put bad guys in jail, where they belong. Sometimes in the cemetery, if they push their luck.

I saw the flash of blue lights, Andy being pulled over. Lisa was straight on the bullhorn. "Mandated sobriety test. Turn off the vehicle, take out the keys and step over here."

For me, it was a matter of about two hundred paces, gun already drawn and ready in my right hand. I always acted on my instinct, and seeing Andy in an unfamiliar ride had set off all kinds of alarms. He hadn't driven anything other than his son's Dodge Ram since he'd been killed in action. That Ford sure as heck wasn't his style, or anywhere within the budget of his lifestyle either.

About twenty feet from the Ford, I took a knee. "Hey, in the car. Wildlife and Fisheries officer here. I am armed. You're covered on both sides, so I suggest you come quietly. Exit the vehicle, hands above your head. Don't try anything silly, or I will use lethal force." I didn't legally have to inform a suspect of my intentions, but I wanted to cover my ass, in case anything went south in a hurry. The trouble with this job, you never knew if today was your last day in uniform. Hell, your last day sucking oxygen in and out, even.

I had to wait. I hate waiting. Actually, I hate a lot of things, but waiting is certainly well up near the top of the list. Along with scumbags and folks who waste my time. "We know you're in there. I'll give you until the count of ten. And then I'm tossing a CS grenade through the door. Save us both the hassle. Whatever you've done, it ain't worth dying for, okay?"

Mississippi. The second longest river in the good old US of A. Also, a great way to count an entire second. I'd shouted out my eighth Mississippi when he finally showed.

"I'm coming out. Don't shoot, man! I'm not armed." In his twenties, probably. There was something about youth which made you feel indestructible, caused you to make bad decisions, and do incredibly dumb-ass things. Mostly for money. Sometimes for drugs. Frequently, significant others were the root course. In this case, it turned out to be a combo platter. "I've got a joint in my jacket pocket. I was taking it to my old lady, for her back pain. Do you know how it is, man? When you love someone, you'll do anything for them."

Yeah, I knew how that song went. Still, we did the usual dance. Hands on the vehicle as I searched him with one hand. "You got any weapons? Any needles, something sharp that might cut or nick me?"

He complied. Well, he hardly had any other options, not with two guns pointed at him. "Please, man. I gotta help her. Just let me go. The old man ain't hurt. I never touched him."

I gave him my best line in stern looks. "You got a name, lover boy? Because right now, this is felony kidnapping."

"Mason! He said he had a gun, son. I felt something in my back. Cold metal. Damn near frightened the life out of me." That was Andy, calling from behind the safety of Lisa's checkpoint. Well, that explained why they weren't in his Ram. It certainly would have taken the threat of actual death to get Andy to leave that truck anywhere he couldn't see it.

A couple of firmer pats found it. Then I needed to stand back for a few seconds. He wasn't going to know I didn't have him covered. He could probably see Lisa pointing her piece at him though. So hopefully he wasn't about to do anything stupid while I quickly got some latex gloves on to actually take the gun off him. Luger. 9 millimeter. It felt real. Until I tried to check if it was loaded. Just a hunk of solid, useless metal. Well, not quite useless. He'd managed to take an old man against his will with the thing.

One thing I hadn't found though. "You got any ID? Driver's license, anything with your name on?"

"No, man. It's not like I was coming out to rob a fool. I just needed someone to help me get the weed over the state line. Hardly like I'm gonna carry any ID as I commit a damn felony, was it?"

He had a point there. "So it was premeditated then?"

"Pre what now?" America. This was your tax dollars at work. I guess he hadn't taken much advantage of the education system.

"You decided to do this before you came out, and brought the replica with you to use to scare people? Yes or no?"

"Yes."

That was all I needed. I could see Lisa making hand signs off to my left. She had already run his plate through dispatch. I left her handcuffing him to the bridge and reading his rights, as I drove Andy back to his truck.

●

On the whole, people in these parts were good, honest, law-abiding folks.

I hate to say that most of the criminals seemed to be from out of state, but you simply cannot argue with cold, hard statistics. Well, you can, but you won't win. I'd check vehicles entering the state. Lisa was stationed on the other side of the river, checking the folks who were leaving.

Normally one in every thirty, unless I got a bad feeling. It was mostly issuing tickets, with the odd warning here and there. If we had to seize anything edible, it would be donated to the needy. There was no shortage of them. Someone somewhere is always going hungry. One time, we stopped a guy with over a hundred rainbow trout. Took it to a local community center. A lot of nice people had themselves a good old-fashioned fish bake that evening. Lisa and I stopped by for a bite. It would have been rude not to, frankly.

I guess you want to know how it happened then? How we died?

I recall it was late into July, the heat had become mighty oppressive. People were doing some really stupid stuff. Every other stop seemed to result in a ticket. It had just passed noon, we got a call from the state police on the north side of the river. A suspect was fleeing, heading in our direction with no sign of stopping. A case of gas and dash, only he'd held up the cashier with a gun too.

In a lime green Dodge Viper, he had probably been stopping every fifty miles to gas up and just got sick of paying. Or the sun had boiled his brain beyond the point of breaking. They didn't have a helicopter in the area yet, no budget for it. Let me tell you this much. It's amazing how quickly Uncle Sam ponies up a whole mess of money after federal employees die in the line of duty.

It's just a shame that the folks who had to die were us. Yours truly, and my partner Lisa. I was going to ask her to marry me when we got off shift. Yep. That very day. The worst day of my life, and the last too. Had the ring in my pocket and everything. Because I knew she felt the same way. Regret is not a great way to spend your afterlife.

Anyway, our suspect vehicle came barreling around a corner and made a J turn onto the bridge. Where young Lee Marsden was riding across on his brand new Huffy. He hadn't quite got the feel for the beast yet, and it went sliding from underneath him.

Directly in front of the oncoming Viper. How he made that flick of his steering wheel, barely missing young master Marsden, I do not know. What I do know? We had been barely feet behind when I saw the kid. With zero chance of braking in time, and even less odds of getting by the kid without turning him into human mincemeat, I only had one other course of action left. I pulled my wheel as hard right as I could, pounding my brakes for all I was worth.

The rest, as they say, is history.

Things I can confirm. There is no light to go towards. You don't have your entire life flash in front of your eyes before you die. You just die. Our brakes weren't great. We were already three months overdue for a full service on the pick-up. It had to get done the next day. Both of us were off duty then. As for the whole unfinished business causing ghosts? I can't honestly say. Sure. I had a girl and wanted to marry her. Never got to tell her. At least not while we were both still upright and breathing the good air of Louisiana, I didn't. That was the only real unfinished business I had left. Apart from living the rest of my life, of course.

My advice? Fulfil your dreams. Don't wait until the right time rolls around. The best time is right now. Live for today, because tomorrow is never guaranteed.

2023

About thirty years ago, there was a memorial sign right here. Only souvenir hunters stole it. And now no-one remembers our names. Most folks barely even remember the movie being made. A lot of those involved are dead now. Like us. That's how life goes. Death too, I guess. It's a nice place to haunt though.

There used to be an advertising board on this side of the river. We'd often park the pick-up behind it and pretend there wasn't anyone on patrol. Some darn fool drove a semi through it about two years ago, he'd fallen asleep at the wheel, too many hours on the road, and not enough rest stops.

Jimmy frequently reminds me how he should have stopped at that Gas 'N Gulp ten miles back for a coffee.

Folks still see us, now and then. The way I understand it, there's a heightened perception, possibly caused by increased blood flow to the brain. Even if they don't see us, some still can hear me shouting "Game Warden!" now and then. Maybe one time in every two or three hundred.

I'm getting weaker by the day. There'll be a time soon when they don't see us again.

So until that day? We're on patrol at Copperhead Bridge. Twenty-four-seven, three-sixty-five. Crime never rests, and neither will we.

Stay out of trouble, you hear me?

Skinning Bone

Brent Salish

"I'd give my left arm for another hit record."

"Hard to play guitar that way." I laughed even as I spoke, though if Charli Enright's fingers had been webbed, her playing wouldn't have suffered significantly. People bought her records and downloaded her tracks for her voice and her songs rather than her minimal competency on her 1950s Martin D-28.

Voice and songs.

Problem was, cigarettes and touring had wreaked revenge on the former, and she hadn't written a truly great song in thirty years.

Some issues a good producer could fix, but those weren't among them.

On the other hand, I had a few tricks up my sleeve. "How much *would* you give for a hit?"

"Extra points?" Points represented percentages of income from a recording. "I'd take some of a lot rather than all of nothing."

"Not talking money." I waved to take in the state-of-the-art recording studio in which we sat, a room that had spawned a dozen platinum albums and at least twenty tunes you could name after the first four notes. Skinning Bone Studios sat on a hundred acres of red-rock scrubland, eight crow-flight miles southwest of Sedona and eight hundred miles from worldly care. "I'm cursed with everything I need and most anything I could want."

I walked over to a beat-to-crap upright piano that was the tonal equivalent of Rod Stewart's voice, utterly imperfect and unreservedly glorious. I played a verse of a slow blues, just a I-IV-V progression that exported a lifetime of pain without a single word.

"Songs become hits for two reasons. Sometimes they just capture the imagination of a moment. A fun two minutes and thirty seconds of ephemeral pleasure. Or seven minutes and fifty-five seconds, in the case of 'Stairway to Heaven'." I played the opening riff on the piano before turning my head toward her. "The other way is when they capture an emotion beyond our understanding." I arpeggiated a D minor chord while continuing to look her in the eyes. "How would you describe the color red to a blind person?"

She shrugged. "I don't know." Her attitude disclosed that she was too old for either dorm-room questions or beer-drinking games.

"I don't know either." I chose not to match her shrug. "But that's what great songs do. They make real those things we only *thought* we imagined. Mostly pain."

"They're not all about pain." She thought for a second.

She grabbed her guitar from the Hercules stand next to her chair, fingered an A minor chord, stared at her fingers without sounding a note. "Jenny here used to call to me a lot more urgently." Her voice was a whisper, audible to me only because of the studio's impeccable acoustics.

She stroked the upper bout of her beloved Jenny, warm rosewood rubbed free of polish across tens of thousands of hours. She breathed deep, and again, and began to fingerpick. Still seated, she sang the first verse of one of the songs she'd brought to the session, then tenderly returned the Martin to the stand. "Lost love. Pain enough for you?"

"You're *acting* the emotion." The song was fine. Perfectly usable album filler, but unconvincing. "Rather than living it."

"I was just running the melody for you." She stood up, strapped on the guitar, and strode to one of the mics. "When I sing it for real, that's when I feel it."

I shook my head, pointed her back to her seat. "I mean the lyrics, the music, everything. You can't sing *into* the song what you never *wrote* into it in the first place." I held her eyes until she sat down, guitar a shield against what I had to say. "I'll ask again. What are you prepared to sacrifice for a *great* song?"

"Anything." Not a moment's hesitation.

"Anything." I spun back to the keyboard and ambled into another blues, minor key this time, from which I segued seamlessly into the chorus of "Skinning Bone," my one semi-hit record as a performer, top ten only by virtue of social-climbing to number nine for a week on the Billboard Hot 100. "My wife died forty years ago this month. That was her story. Well, my story, really." Indescribable pain, of which I'd captured but a proportion, yet a sliver sharp enough to draw blood from anyone who listened honestly to the song.

I stopped playing, fingers hovering above the keys until my heart rate settled.

I turned back to Charli. "Let's take a walk."

She grabbed her cigarettes, lit up once we got outside.

"I hear lung cells dying." I led her toward the rise behind the studio. "This was the clearest air in Arizona until thirty seconds ago."

"You will *not* make me feel guilty. Besides, I can still smell the residue from the fires last fall."

"I'm not sure."

"I've been nicotining for fifty years and if *I* can smell it, you certainly can." She dragged on her smoke, then extinguished the butt on the sole of her sneaker, pinched the ash end with her fingers, opened her pack and dropped it in. "Figured you wouldn't want me littering."

"Figured right."

We walked another twenty steps in silence before I realized she had stopped, was no longer beside me.

She drew a deep breath through her nose. "You mean you really can't smell the…? I don't know. Burned. Something rotting."

"I smell it. Just not from the fires, is all." I tossed my head at the path still ahead of us, barely visible in the thin dirt, and walked on without checking to be sure she was following.

She was.

At the top of the rise, she put her hand on my shoulder, breathing hard. "Wait a sec. I don't have the lung power I used to. And don't say anything."

So I didn't, even though I might have mentioned the altitude, almost a mile above sea level. Instead, I gazed out toward the sparse low bushes a few hundred yards beyond.

A footbridge spanned the bare patch, dark and weathered wood fifteen inches above the dusky ground. The structure was almost invisible, as if the otherwise lacerating sunlight had been coerced to bend around rather than illuminate the bridge and the plot of desert beneath.

She spotted the bridge after a few seconds. "Where's that go?"

I strained to see through the shadows that darkened the footbridge despite the brilliant late-April noonday sun. "Let's see. If you're willing."

"As long as it's downhill." She pulled out another cigarette, caught the look in my eye, returned it to the pack. Then defiantly shook it free again and lit up. "I'd rather smell this than…whatever. The fires."

I slowed our pace as we descended toward the bridge, timing our walk so that she finished her smoke well before we reached the heavy wooden structure.

Freud—or Jung or maybe Wikipedia—could have used the span to illustrate an approach-avoidance conflict. Forty years, and I still found myself drawn closer even as the skin and bone of my body resisted further strides.

Charli wrinkled her nose against the odor, emanating from no specific location but nonetheless hovering as if the bridge were in a vale rather than on level ground. "This goes…nowhere," with a head-point toward the structure.

I knew exactly where it went.

I'd built it in the months after I'd lost Susan, laboriously dragging four-by-fours and two-by-sixes and rough-hewn logs and concrete pier blocks up and over the hill. I'd staged the materials in the driveway of what we'd believed was our forever home, back when the studio was three mics, a piano, two amps, a minimalist drum kit and an early eight-track digital audio recorder, all crammed into what we'd expected to repurpose as the baby's room.

With hand tools only, I'd sawed and notched and joined—and bled and blistered, sweated and sunburned—until I had created an inelegant but sturdy crossing that allowed me to pass over the barren ground without making contact. Selected clients, too, might make that passage. "It may not go where you expect, no."

She took a step, hesitated, then edged to the side. "Is this like some arroyo thing?" She pointed with the hand holding her cigarettes at the unvegetated ground. "Flash floods?"

I swept my hand across the uniform landscape before us.

She followed my point. "No. It's all level, isn't it?" She suppressed a frisson, probably without realizing she'd done so. "Does it ever rain here?"

"Occasionally."

"Cause it's all dead." Even though, a few hundred feet beyond, the scrub resumed, low trees, juniper and ponderosa, along with yucca and, in the distance, where my acreage butted up against the national forest, a stand of prickly pear.

I forced myself closer to the bridge. "Anything," I repeated, my eyes locking with hers. "For a great record. Anything." Already I could feel the pull, the murky energy prickling my skin.

"What *haven't* I given? My life. My voice. My lungs, as you say. Three husbands. Two sexual assaults, if you must know. You're a guy, so at least you didn't have to give *that*."

She coughed hard into her elbow, then spit phlegm, instinctively turning away, not from me, but from the bridge. "If you want to sleep with me…" She made the half-offer still facing back up the rise.

"There's no good way to answer that, is there?"

"There is not." She faced me again, a slight smile dying on her lips. "But—"

"That's not what I'm asking."

"You never remarried, did you?"

Avoiding my question. Everyone did, at first. So I answered hers. "No." I couldn't. Had never considered the idea, the impossible notion. I glanced over my shoulder. Maybe this wasn't the day, nor Charli the right client. "We could head back."

She made no attempt to leave, to climb the ragged hill and seek the refuge of the studio beyond, nor did she walk toward the future I was clearly asking her to contemplate. Instead, she crouched, scooped a few ounces of pebbles and dirt, let them run through her fingers. "Skinning bone. That wasn't a misheard expression. Was it?"

Such was the story I'd articulated for forty years, or at least as long as fans and deejays and writers and even clients continued to ask me about that song. Here, by the foot of the bridge, no lies were tolerated, not even the lies we tell ourselves. "No." I didn't elaborate.

"Broken love is like a bone bruise. That's how I've always heard it. Scraped and bleeding, and then for two weeks you can't even touch it, all raw and purple." She stood again and gazed without seeing, at a grouping of scruffy ponderosa. "I was running in the woods once, and tripped and fell hard against a log. I thought I'd die from the pain, even though I knew of course I wouldn't."

Bone bruise, all right. Close enough. I saw no reason to correct her. To prolong her stalling.

She focused again, looked me in the eye. "Because I'd go through that again." Rubbed at her hip. "A hundred times."

"Worse."

She snorted. "You're saying that if I walk that bridge, I'll have a hit record. And pay for it, somehow."

"You'll find a great song. Write one, snatch it out of the ether, channel heaven or hell, wherever those songs actually come from. And together, we'll make it so that people stop and listen. So they *have* to listen, because it hurts even more not to listen. But a hit? That takes PR flacks and the right deejays and Spotify playlists and absolute luck. I can't promise that part."

"I've got a team that can handle their end. They made 'Rooftop Loving' enough to build a tour around, and it was *not* a great song. Catchy, but...What did you call it earlier? Ephemeral." She furrowed her brow, tilted her head in confusion. Or in challenge. "Wait. How is 'Stairway' ephemeral?"

"Not the song. The transient emotions it evokes. Though to be honest, I'd listen to Robert Plant sing the phone book."

"Isn't picking words from the phone book how he wrote 'The Immigrant Song'?" She managed a faint smile, then opened her mouth—undoubtedly an impulse to sing the 'aah-aah-aah...ah!' opening—before closing it without a sound. Even for a born singer, the sense of shadow near the bridge suppressed all music.

She squinted up at the sun, unbearably splendid overhead, then back to the barren patch that sunlight struggled to reach. She pressed her lips together, mumbled, "I want that song."

I didn't respond.

"Anything." She raised her head, met my eyes. "I'll give anything. I want—I need that song." She took three slow steps until she stood abreast of the piers of the footbridge.

"Wait." I took a deep breath, then another. "We walk together." I shuddered.

Unlike her, I knew what lay ahead.

And I wanted that song nearly as much as she did. To make her again not just memorable but inevitable, unstoppable. "Walk ahead of me. Stay in the middle."

"It's not going to collapse, is it?"

"It'll hold an elephant." Maybe only a baby elephant, but I'd built it sturdy. I'd built to outlast not just me but my memories. I'd built so that when Charli lost her balance, when she collapsed into the vortexes of pain, she'd tumble to the bridge rather than the ground beneath. My planks would support her. The earth would not.

I rested my palm on her shoulder and moved with her, in part to remain in contact, but also to ensure she kept moving at a measured pace until I could guide her fall.

Her shoulder twitched and the muscles in her neck tightened, which is when I knew she heard them. I too heard them.

Of course I did, because how could I not? That anguish *would* be heard, would not be denied. A sound I'd lived with for forty years, agony that would not release me, an upwelling of grief hot and rancid as the magma sprinting toward freedom through a volcano's vent.

Yet my pain was but a fraction of the agony suffusing the terrain beneath and filling every crevice of the souls of those who dared walk above, displacing all joy and mirth as we goaded fate by strutting through the living's realm.

Join me, she sang.

You put me here, she howled.

I never had a chance, he shrieked.

His voice. I dreaded that sound most of all.

Through shadow and tears, I lost all vision, held desperately to Charli's shoulder as she wobbled, as she fell, as I guided her to the planed wood, tumbling forward with her, atop her, shielding her from the sun even as the wails rose from beneath.

You promised, she roared, and I had no words, for I had indeed promised, we had promised each other. Susan, I tried, I tried so hard to keep my promise, and at the end it was all I could do not to throw myself into your grave and let the earth consume us both.

But you didn't.

Someone had to keep your memory alive. To wrest value from loss. To make your death mean something.

And mine, he sobbed. *You never even gave me a name.*

How could I name what I never knew? Susan and I planned to name you only when we saw you, only when...

Only when I cut you free, skinning bone and flesh with a goddam kitchen knife, knowing I'd lost Susan, trying to rescue *you* while screaming at God and berating the books and cursing my stupidity in believing that people were built to deal with whatever happened, forcing my breath between sobs to inflate your tiny lungs, until the spectral moon glared down at a shattered nativity and whispered, *Enough.* Murmured, *Now you have a new task.*

It was the moon once again, a crescent this time trailing the setting sun, that guided Charli and me off the bridge. We huddled together in the dry dirt beyond, blind and crushed, our souls splintered, crazed and cracked, riven by crevasses that could be plugged—if at all—only by music.

Charli clutched my shoulders, sobbing. "Do we...have to cross back?"

There would be no crossing back.

I led her the long way around, up the hill, toward refuge.

Her voice was low at first, a barely audible croak, distorted by shivering in the cold desert evening, as she groped for the notes, teased out the words.

We entered the studio, which crouched unlit.

Even within the darkness, Charli was drawn unerringly to her guitar.

Underneath

Jean Jentilet

I grew up a short drive (or a brave walk) from Governor's Bridge, a little steel blip on a back road between Annapolis and Bowie. The history books say that Governor's Bridge was so named because it was built by one of Maryland's early governors to give him a shortcut from the capital to his private home. That's the official story. But we all know the *other* stories. Little one-lane country bridges—even if it's a little less country every day—breed stories like rotten food breeds maggots.

One of the old favorites is about a Cold War science experiment at a secret military base, the usual attempt to defy the laws of nature and make a super soldier. The thing the experimenters ended up with was part man and part goat, a murderous, insensible beast that slaughters anyone who gets in its way after dark.

Then there's the one about that tragic prom night in the 1950s when two cars full of drunk and happy prom-goers—one coming from Bowie, one coming from Annapolis—met in the middle of the bridge, each going full speed. There wasn't much left of the cars, and even less left of the kids, but the bridge remained, and if you're on the bridge at midnight on prom night (which school's prom night, the legend doesn't say) you can hear car tires clawing for traction, and the screams of those kids careening towards their deaths.

Of course, there are the murders. So many murders. Some of them go back even further than the official story, like the stable hand who hung the maid who had spurned his advances. Their master discovered the crime just as the stable hand was dropping the maid's body into the river. If you find yourself at the bridge after the last traces of the sun have left the sky, and you're very quiet and still, you can hear the splash of her body hitting the water.

There are countless stories of jealous husbands, treacherous business partners, and children looking to collect their inheritances early. If you're at the bridge at dusk or midnight or three in the morning, on this day or another day or any day, and if you sit in a certain spot, or turn off your flashlight, or light a candle with a match, or say a particular phrase, you can see them or hear them. Their fights and their cries and the sounds of their dying breaths.

These are the stories everyone tells each other, the stories everyone adds their own little flourishes to, the stories everyone laughs about even as they look over their shoulders. But I know the real story.

My father worked a lot, so most of the time we spent together was on weekends in the spring and summer. I would spend Friday night making sandwiches and cutting up apples, while Dad sorted out lines and poles in the garage, and on Saturday morning, we'd pack it all into the back of the minivan and head out to Governor's Bridge. Dad and I would spend most of the day out there, and if the weather held and the fish were biting, we'd stay out until gnats swarmed thick over the water, and lightning bugs twinkled in the dusky woods like stars. Once in a while, we even caught something big enough for dinner, though that was never the point. We always left before full dark. Dad never said as much out loud, but I think that all the old stories got under his skin a little, too.

The bridge is a different place at night. I learned that the hard way during a sleepover at my friend Daryl's house. Daryl's family had been around since before the bridge, and their old farmhouse, like the other old farmhouses in the area, could almost fit into the garage of the new houses sprouting up around it on one-acre lots like high-foyered mushrooms.

As a kid growing up in one of those mushrooms, I liked the sense of adventure of all the acres of forgotten woods at Daryl's. His family even had a graveyard going back to the 1600s on the back of their property. It was weedy and ringed with poison ivy, and most of the inscriptions were worn down to the faintest impressions of names or years or prayers. At the end of the cemetery farthest from Daryl's house there was a rectangular section marked off by four knee-high, square stones. The grass in that whole area stayed yellow, even in the summer, and its whole perimeter dipped towards its center, where you could just make out a smooth, flat rock that went on under the yellow grass in every direction.

One time, Daryl's mother told us that some old witches from colonial times had been buried there in unmarked graves, with bricks in their mouths to keep them from coming up out of the ground. She said that the whole thing had to be filled in every few years to stop bones from poking up through the dirt, until finally, Daryl's great-great-great-great grandfather had that big, flat rock hauled over the whole mess. Daryl's mother might have been just trying to scare us off the whole area, but we didn't stop going back there. We just stayed away from that spot. None of us wanted to find out the hard way that it wasn't just a story.

Going to Governor's Bridge was our friend Greg's idea. His mother had gotten him a video camera for his birthday. Greg never met his father, and all he really knew about him was that he'd been a cameraman and had worked on a lot of movies. He'd been on the set of one when an explosion he was filming blew the wrong way. His mom used the settlement from the studio to give Greg anything he wanted, and he wanted to be Ridley Scott, or James Cameron, or even just the father he had never met, and so she got him the camera. He got it into his head that we could go out to Governor's Bridge and take videos, and maybe we would see something or hear something, and we could get proof on tape. Somebody would pay money for it, Greg said. It'd be all over the news. We'd be rich.

It was the middle of summer, so by the time the sun went down, it was getting late anyway. The three of us sat in Daryl's room playing video games until we were sure that his parents were in for the night. We snuck out through the mudroom, Greg carrying his camera, Daryl with a flashlight in his pocket and his pellet air rifle slung over his shoulder, and me one-arming a backpack full of soda and snacks.

The full moon cast deep shadows along the edge of the woods that bordered the property. Frogs and crickets and all of the other things that come out at night filled the air with their chatter. We went out to the back field, within view of the family cemetery, where silhouettes of gravestones stood against the nightglow like something from an old black and white horror movie. Then we stepped into the woods.

At first, the trees were thin enough that we could see each other and where we were going by moonlight, but the deeper we went, the darker and cooler and quieter it became, until the moon was just scraps of light sneaking between the trees, and my skin crawled with goosebumps. The frogs and crickets and everything else fell to a distant murmur behind the crunch and snap of leaves and dead branches under our feet.

"Turn on a light," Greg hissed.

"Don't you have one on that camera?" Daryl asked.

"Saving battery for the bridge. Just turn on a light, numbnuts."

Daryl gave his flashlight a shake, then switched it on. It was good to have the light, even if it didn't give us much to see but trees and more trees. The tangles of branches that looked all the same to me made sense to him, and he didn't once stop to get his bearings even as we got so deep that I began to wonder if we were going in the wrong direction. Before too much longer, the night songs of frogs and crickets swallowed our footsteps again, and the soft babble of water down a well-known path over well-worn rocks joined in harmony. The beam of Daryl's flashlight landed on a snarled knot in the fork of a tree trunk.

"Almost there," Daryl said, and then we were back out in the moonlight, steps from the river. I was careful to watch where he stepped. I had slipped into the river enough times with Dad to know how tricky the footing could be. Also, if I kept my eyes on Daryl's feet, it was easier to ignore the dark movements out of the corner of my eye. The luminous gray skeleton of the bridge came into view, one bone at a time: the truss, the end piece, the deck. When the sun went down, it took the quiet little country bridge with it, and the moon replaced it with this looming, grinning hulk. In the dense void under the bridge, two yellow embers drifted from just above the water, then stopped and hovered just below the deck.

Fireflies.

Their movement was smooth for fireflies, and they stayed maybe a hand's width apart and level with each other. Not so much like fireflies, but they couldn't be anything else.

Couldn't be.

"We're supposed to sit under it, right?" Greg raised the camera to his face. The little red light above the lens shimmered.

"Where's your light?" I asked.

"Trying to shoot in the moonlight. I figured the ghosts or whatever wouldn't like the regular light. And also, ambience. You know?"

Daryl turned around. "Ambience?"

"Yeah, you don't get it. I know."

Daryl glanced up at the sky, then both ways up and down the river. "At midnight, we can hear the prom car, right?"

"On prom night," Greg said. "Which was last month."

"But a lot of stuff happens at midnight," I said. "Like those two kids that the guy from Crownsville got."

This was another old favorite that everyone knew. A maniac had escaped one of the old asylums, and then found two teenagers pulled over at the shoulder one night. When the boy got out to take a leak, the maniac used a scalpel he'd cadged from the hospital to slash the boy's throat. When the girl got out to see what was taking so long, the maniac slit her throat, too. Then he sat their bloodless corpses up in the middle of the bridge, cold hand in cold hand. If you start across the bridge with your headlights off at midnight, then turn them on just before you hit the middle, you'll see the misty shapes of their bodies slumped shoulder to shoulder, and you'll hear the girl's scream just before the killer's scalpel silences it for good.

"My mom said she's pretty sure she saw them one night. The kids, not the killer," Daryl said. "I heard you're supposed to sit in the middle of the bridge, right? And then you see their headlights?"

Greg lowered the camera and shook his head. "I never heard that. That sounds like something else. It also sounds like a good way to get creamed. How do you know if they're ghost headlights or regular headlights?"

Daryl mumbled something that the chorus of bugs shouted down. Greg's teeth phosphoresced in the moonlight as a smile spread across his face.

"Didn't they used to burn witches at the stake out here or something? Like all those bodies buried in your backyard, D?"

Daryl and I traded a look.

"No," Daryl said.

"No way," I said.

"Wussies." Greg snickered, then started up the bank, camera clutched in one hand, stabilizing himself with the other hand on the ground. At the top of the bank, he turned back to us. "You wussies coming or what?"

"We have to go back soon," Daryl grumbled, but followed Greg's path all the same.

A cool, soft breeze picked up once we all three had solid feet on the shoulder where the truss tapered into the ground. Greg lifted his camera back up to his face.

"One of us should go to the other end, then one of us in the middle, and one of us on this end. If a *real* car comes, we can get out of the way."

"Whatever," Daryl said, but didn't move.

I didn't move either. Being up there on the bridge—tree limbs rasping beams, girders moaning through secret rust—wasn't the same light panic as riding a roller coaster. It was heavy, and I could feel it on me, all over me in a filthy sweat. Even breathing didn't feel right.

"Well, we can't all be down here," Greg said. "That won't do anything."

I wanted to go back to the house and eat some of the junk in my backpack, maybe watch some movies. R movies that my parents would never let me watch at home. So, I did something I'd never done before: I called Greg's bluff.

"Then you go. I'll go to the middle, you go down there."

His smile slipped a little. Just a little. "Yeah, let's do it."

I snugged up the straps on my backpack and smacked Daryl's arm. "Got your flashlight?"

Greg tugged my arm before Daryl had a chance to answer. "Let's go."

Stepping onto the bridge was like climbing onto the back of a living thing. As soon as my foot landed on that first grate, a charge went through me, like touching a doorknob in the winter but sharper, and through my whole body at once. I thought of the pair of fireflies rising in the dark below us. Greg was half a dozen steps ahead of me when he stopped hard and turned towards me. The red light on his camera glared an accusation.

"Wussing out now? Really? Now?"

Behind me, Daryl shuffled his feet. Maybe he was thinking what I was, that Greg was acting *wrong*. He was acting out of place. Something had changed, and he was the only one who didn't know it.

"I'm coming," I said.

We walked, the bridge's steel bones shivering under our feet. As we neared the halfway point—the fateful halfway point, where so many stories met—the realization crept in on me, one breath at a time, that the frogs and the bugs and the breeze were all going about their night beyond the bridge, *outside* of the bridge. Their sounds muffled and slid away from the bridge's sides like pebbles across ice before disappearing into silence. If I turned at that moment, I knew—I didn't think, I *knew*—that Daryl would be standing stock still, frozen where we had left him. Because everything that was not on the bridge had stopped. Greg and I were the only things in the world still moving.

But that was impossible.

I watched Greg's back. It was all in my mind. Psychosomatic, Dad would say, like a stomachache on the morning of a math test. Greg would get to the end of the bridge, and nothing would happen, and we would go back to the house and eat snacks and watch R movies.

I guess I had my mind set on how I wanted things to go, so I don't know how long I was actually looking at *it* before my mind registered what my eyes were seeing. A fraction of a moment stretched out like chewed gum pulling off a hot sidewalk, and in that fraction, my mind watched itself work. Watched itself see something, see something was wrong, then see what was wrong. And then that moment collapsed back into its rightful place.

There was something at the other end of the bridge.

Fireflies.

Two fireflies, floating at the same level a hand's width apart. They shone through an iridescent gray-white veil, like distant headlights on a foggy night.

Fireflies.

I wanted to believe that.

Fireflies.

I knew better.

A deep, solid blackness rose up behind them like a wave closing in on a hapless surfer. I was sweating and shivering all at once, my mouth full of bile and cotton, but I couldn't look away.

"Hey," I said, swiping Greg's arm with my fingertips.

"I know," Greg answered, voice low, camera to his face, not moving. Something had finally triggered his survival instinct. "Just..." The word tightened around whatever he was holding back—panic, the urge to run. The camera shifted in his hand. "Just wait."

Greg stepped forward. And then the mist and the fireflies and the black wave weren't at the end of the bridge anymore, but just on the other side of the halfway point. They didn't move there. There were no gray-white or dim yellow streaks, no flurry of movement, no footsteps, no roar of a bleak and bottomless ocean of night. They were just there.

I wanted to say Greg's name. I wanted to grab his arm. I wanted to run. It all seemed hopeless. Pointless. We would never outrun whatever we were seeing. We just stood watching, not understanding, not knowing what else to do. The light from the viewer of Greg's camera glowed on, unfazed. We had evidence. We had proof. And we'd never get off the bridge to show it to anyone.

From inside the darkness just beyond the fireflies, something pinged off the deck. And again, clear and strong, this time from somewhere between us and the thing, and then the back of my calf stung and burned. The veil shuddered and the wave shrunk and the fireflies flickered, and then they were halfway back to where they had started on the other side of the bridge. No movement. Just there. Greg's free arm swung down to his side. Another ping, farther down the bridge again.

I blinked, and there was nothing on the bridge but me and Greg and the night. The fireflies weren't gone, though. I couldn't see them anymore, but I knew there in my stomach, there in my bones, that they were nearby, maybe back under the bridge. Greg must have felt it, too, because he didn't run either. We both walked backwards, towards Daryl. I kept Greg in my peripheral vision, not taking my focus off the end of the bridge. I imagined the fireflies floating in their mist, back into our moment, our space, their dark wave breaking over us, swirling around us.

I didn't turn until I felt the gravel of the road under my shoes. Daryl stood with his air rifle still braced against his shoulder, its scope to his eye, and didn't lower it until both of Greg's feet were on solid ground as well.

The pain in my calf soared. I reached down and touched it and winced. The spot was tender, but the skin wasn't broken.

"Ricochet," Daryl said, turning away, slinging the rifle back onto his shoulder. "I didn't mean—"

"Barely felt it," I lied.

We started down the road towards Daryl's house, staying on the slim shoulder. It would take longer—a lot longer—than going back through the woods. Even with the bugs and frogs working to outdo each other's calls, it was too quiet. Greg's shoes scraped the shoulder as he kicked a stray bit of crumbled asphalt out in front of him. Chip bags crinkled when I shifted my backpack from shoulder to shoulder. Daryl sighed a lot, and when we were a little more than halfway back to the house, he spoke.

"You know, Dad said once the new starter comes in, his old four-wheeler'll be ready to go. We should take it out to the track."

"I have soccer camp after next week," Greg said, not looking up from his asphalt.

Daryl glanced over his shoulder at me. I shrugged.

"We're going to the beach. I don't know when," I said.

Daryl nodded. "Yeah. Okay."

No one said another word until we got back to the house. In the mudroom, we had just kicked off our shoes when Daryl reached out and tapped the camera's lens cover. Greg looked down at the camera strapped around his hand as if he'd forgotten it was there. He shook his head.

"I don't know, man. I think…I think I just want to watch some movies or something. I mean, it needs to charge and these tapes won't fit your VCR, so…you know."

"Movies sound good to me, too," I said, trying not to sound relieved.

Daryl shrugged and nodded. "Sure. Movies sound good."

We spread out in the living room and ate the snacks from my backpack and watched movies. Greg's camera sat on an end table in the corner, red light blinking to show it was plugged in and charging. I fell into a thin and noisy sleep before it turned a steady, full-charge green. I didn't dream.

When I woke up a few hours later Daryl was still asleep, but Greg was sitting at the kitchen table, his camera resting between his hands with its viewer open like a one-winged bird.

"It isn't there," he said. He slid the camera to the center of the table. "We saw it, man. I know we saw it."

I nodded. I couldn't make him stop talking about it, but I didn't have to say anything myself.

Greg straightened up in his chair, then reached over and snapped the viewer closed. "But if the camera didn't see it…"

He never finished that sentence, and I didn't ask any more about it. The truth is that if his camera had caught anything that night, things would be different. (For me, anyway.) As it was, my mind did what minds do: it smoothed over the sharpest edges of the memory, and let time do the rest of the work.

I decided that whatever we saw had more to do with what we wanted to see than anything actually happening that night. So, when my father proposed a day of fishing at the bridge a few weeks later, I didn't hesitate. The promise of a Saturday lazing on the banks scuffed away the last rough spots still poking out from that night.

Dad and I picked up donuts on the way out, ate half of them and tossed the rest into the cooler packed with the sandwiches I had made the night before.

We pulled off onto the shoulder as close to the bridge as we could get like always and grabbed our gear. There were a handful of cars parked along the shoulder and down by the canoe launch. Along the banks a few other people had already set their gear and were crouched on their haunches or settled into tent chairs to watch their lines. It was a perfect morning, really. Birds sang and bees buzzed and butterflies fluttered by.

I was halfway down the bank before I realized I was walking Greg's path from the night of the sleepover. I turned the thought over in my mind once, maybe twice, but in the end, we weren't even all the way down to the water's edge before I decided that I had a whole Saturday ahead of me, and that was all that mattered. There was a family with two little kids on a big blanket in our usual spot. Dad and I headed to the next best section of the bank. It was a clearing low against the river, with a wide flat patch that was good for sorting out gear, and a fallen tree that stayed shaded most of the day and was perfect for kicking back with lunch. I put the cooler down on the tree, then helped Dad with the gear.

We cast our lines out and reeled them in, and cast them out and reeled them in, each cast and reel different than the one before, and also the same. Up and down the river, the gentle splashes of lures hitting water dotted the air. The sun trudged its path in the sky, and it was just after dawn forever until it wasn't.

"What'd you make us for lunch?" Dad asked, casting out.

"Roast beef." My stomach growled at the words.

"Let's see what this does, then I'm ready to eat."

I watched Dad's line settle in the water, laying there weightless and straight for a minute before drifting down towards the bottom of the river. My bladder made itself known.

"I have to go," I said.

"Okay." Dad gave his line a gentle tug but didn't look away from it.

I rested my pole against the lunch log. If we had been in our usual spot on a usual day, I would have gone behind the closest tree. Out there by the clearing, with so many people around, I didn't have many choices. I started up the bank at the least steep spot I could find. I recognized the tree with the gnarly knot from that night with Greg and Daryl.

This was close to where we had come out of the woods, but all the threat was gone here in the middle of a perfect day. Sun pattered through the trees and settled like a thousand feathers on the underbrush. Shouts and laughter, round and happy, filtered up from the river. I could see pieces of the bridge peeking past the dark green of full trees. Nobody would see me unless they knew where to look and what they were looking for. I turned to step behind the knotty tree, barely noticing the prickling on my skin.

"I know you."

My stomach jumped at the snap of cold air on my cheek and the soft voice near my ear. I spun around.

The man was leaning against a tree fifteen or twenty feet away, slightly downhill and between me and the bridge, his head cocked to the side like a curious puppy, his bright blue eyes unblinking. He was younger than Dad, but I couldn't say by how much. I couldn't say anything about him, like what his clothes looked like or even the color of his hair. Just those big, unblinking blue eyes.

"Okay," I said, and I looked further up the bank for another tree. I had to go. I wanted to be away from him. The surprise of him being there had tilted my mood.

"My name is William Schuyler. You know me as well. I am certain that you do," he said, and with a quiver like his whole body was a flicking wrist, he drifted away from the tree. "Where are your companions?"

Had he been out in the woods that night, down by the river, night fishing or looking for bait? I didn't know the name, no matter what he said. I sorted through all the houses and farms nearby, all the families, all the kids I knew, their older brothers, their fathers. I couldn't place him, and I didn't like him.

"They're at home, I guess," I said. "I'm here with my Dad."

I nodded towards the clearing, towards where Dad was now rifling through the cooler, looking for the sandwich with no mayo. When I looked back, the man was gone as quickly and quietly as he had appeared. I scanned the woods and listened, but I didn't give it any more time than it took me to relieve myself, and then I was moving as fast as I dared through the underbrush and back to the river.

Dad tossed a sandwich towards me just as I broke out of the woods and dropped to a walk.

"Someone chasing you? What's the rush?"

I managed to catch the sandwich, and I think I managed to not sound panicked. I didn't want him to think I was scared, and I didn't want him to ask questions. The blue-eyed man was gone, and I didn't want to think about him.

"Just wanted to get back before you ate the whole cooler."

Dad shook his head and grinned. "You better start making more food then."

Morning became afternoon while we ate, and then we went back to our gear. Dad asked me about my plans for the rest of the summer, and I asked him if he was going to make it to the beach with me and Mom. He said he would try. By then, the fireflies had started to pop out of the dimming sky, and the gnats had begun to gather in their groups over the water.

"I guess it's that time," Dad said, casting out again. "Last one. Whoever reels in first starts packing up."

I was still hoping to catch something, but the woods pressed at my back. The thought of the man who'd come out of nowhere and gone back to it tugged at my gut. "I give up," I said, reeling in my line.

"That's fine." Dad's jaw was set and his eyes were narrowed. He had one of his feelings. His feelings were never wrong. He was going to catch something.

"I'll get the van packed up."

"Yep." Dad's voice was strained. That meant something was nibbling but not quite biting.

I pulled the cooler and the rest of the gear out toward the water to pack it up. Away from the woods. By the time I was headed back towards the bridge, the banks were all but empty. One old man on the opposite bank was pulling down lines he'd had hanging from some tree limbs. We nodded at each other as I passed, and I quickened my pace.

Something felt wrong. It wasn't the old man—he was just a grandad. Night was coming on like a storm, and I worried Dad had lost track of time, and I worried that he expected me to come back to the clearing after I dropped the gear off, and I didn't want to do that. I decided that once I got up to the van, I would just throw everything into the back and then sit and wait.

I was almost to one of the easy sections of the bank, where the way up towards the road wasn't so steep and didn't have so many trees when I saw them, the perfectly paired fireflies, shining out from under the bridge. I started up the bank on the diagonal from where I was, so that I wouldn't have to get too close to the bridge until I was almost to the road.

When I reached the top of the incline, I made my way along the person-wide path, running between the edge of the woods and the bank's drop off, switching the cooler from hand to hand to keep my balance. The van was within sight on the shoulder. A few more steps, and I was at the end of the bridge, where the truss tapered into the road. I switched the cooler one more time, then steadied myself with my free hand on the lip of the bridge's end post as I stepped onto the last few feet of the bridge's deck.

The steel was slick. Slimy. When I tried to pull my hand back, I couldn't move. The old man fidgeting around on the bank below and the frogs burping and bugs nattering all dissolved into a great stillness until the only thing I could hear was my heart.

A thick, bitter smell cluttered the air on a breeze too cold for the end of a perfect summer day. It caught in my throat and crawled into my lungs. Electricity tingled in my fingers and toes. The stillness reached everything—my muscles, my heart, my lungs—like frost spreading across a windshield.

Something crackled in my ears, louder and louder until I was sure my head would explode. I put everything I had into screaming. My jaw muscles twitched and were just managing my mouth open when I blinked. The split second that my eyes were closed swelled into endlessness.

When I opened my eyes, I was near the middle of the bridge. I looked down towards the river. I should have been able to see Dad, but I couldn't. The old man was gone, too, and the van. Bits and pieces of information came in, and I tried to make them all fit but none of them did.

Everything was wrong.

Where the old steel grates should have been under my feet, there were wide, flat logs. There was no truss, just a log, bark peeling, as thick as two men bundled together where guardrails had been before. I spun in place once, twice, but nothing changed. Everything was still wrong. There was a hand on my shoulder. I turned, expecting to see my father. The man standing there was no one I knew, though he looked familiar. His hair and eyes were dark, as black as the cape hanging off the back of his shoulders like folded wings.

"I will not offer another chance for mercy, witch." The low hiss of the man's voice drifted towards me as if it was part of the breeze. "Prove yourself now to be anything but a charlatan. Call upon that old traitor you call your master to testify to your powers, because I have seen no sign that you are anything save a maid thinking herself clever."

Something moved in my throat, like a fist doing somersaults. I tried to speak around it, to tell the man that this was all a mistake or a dream, but nothing made it past the flipping flopping pain.

I turned away from him, stepped away, thinking that if nothing else, I could run, but all of my movements felt like they were through fast-moving water. I turned back towards the man, but it wasn't just him anymore. There was a woman there where I'd been standing, a heavy looking rope wrapped around her waist and holding her arms straight to her sides.

Behind her, another man stood between two horses. The blue-eyed man from the woods.

William Schuyler. I know you.

The big man with the dark hair and eyes towered over all of it. His cape could have swallowed the whole mass of horses and humans with one swoop.

The woman raised her head and looked into the big man's face. He took a step back, and I could see why. Her eyes blazed with hatred like a stoked fire climbing out of a furnace grate.

"Who are you to demand? To question? A man that needs the help of a clever maid to curry favor?" Her voice slithered and slipped around the huffing of the horses. Her tangled dark hair fell around her dirt-splotched face. "He will not come to your call. You will receive what you have paid for. All the sacrifices have been made."

The big man's hand twitched. Something moved in his eyes, but it was nothing I understood. "Have they, truly? All of them?"

In that same moment, the wide-eyed man dropped a loop of rope around the woman's neck. She didn't seem to notice, but the man in the cape smiled.

"I believe, my dear Elizabeth, my clever maid, that there yet remains a sacrifice to be made." He put his face close to the woman's. "You are nothing more than a danger to my good name now." He stepped back from her, then straightened up to his full height. "William! There is a witch among us. What are we called upon to do with witches?"

William yanked up on the rope and started back towards the thick log railing. The woman didn't scream. She spoke instead.

"You. And your children, Jeremiah Falstaff." The last word came out thin and ragged. White spittle flecked her purpling lips. "And their children." William wrapped the rope around the thick log railing. If either man heard her words, they didn't show it. "And their children's children, until the end of days." Each word was smaller than the one before it, and still she went on. "I will see you and the whole of your line in Hell. This very river will bear witness to my promise." The last word died in a whisper.

Jeremiah let out a sharp bark of laughter. "Your failures have given the lie to your fables, witch. Your consort is impotent. Your threats are empty." Without another word, he wrapped his arms around her waist and started towards the railing, pushing her before him as he went.

He pressed her against the railing, pinning her, and then hoisted her up onto the railing by the rope around her waist. She kicked towards his chest, sending him back a step—just a step—before he gave one final push, and she went over the side in a flurry of skirts and rope with a screech ending in a thick, wet snap. Then there was just the water, crooning down its ancient course.

The men looked over the railing, then looked at each other. Something winked in Jeremiah's hand. It was over almost before it began: the blade flashed and then the thin red line, nearly black in the moonlight, running from one ear to the other appeared across William's throat, and a red-black sheet sluiced down his neck. His eyes went even wider as he fell to his knees. Jeremiah stepped towards him, stood over him. "I came upon you having only just murdered my family's maid without cause. You turned on me, your very own master. To cheat your indenture, perhaps." Jeremiah put the sole of a shiny back boot to William's chest and pushed. William fell to the ground, life dribbling out of the wound in his neck and soaking into the logs of the bridge's deck.

All of the sounds of the night—frogs and bugs and breeze and river—slid away. There was only the thin scraping of William's last breaths and the creaking of the rope dangling Elizabeth's corpse over the river. The moment pulled away at the edges, then snapped back.

I was on the bridge. The steel bridge, the one I had always known. Alone. I had just enough time to be relieved despite my confusion when the fireflies rose in their dire mist, through the grates of the bridge, floating so close I could have touched them.

"You are not the one." The voice wrapped around me, pulling up hairs all over my body.

I blinked. The fireflies blinked back, like headlights flickering through fog. Brakes shrieked. A horn wailed. White pain spread out from my gut. I was weightless, and there was a rush of air. Then I was looking at the sky. Everything was warped and blurry. A car engine revved somewhere above me. Cold water pressed around me.

Any second now, I thought, Dad will see me.

Any second now. Any second now.

By the time my father's face appeared above me, my vision had shrunk down to a narrow round spot just big enough to see him dimly. I could still hear him choke on his shock, and then scream.

He sat there in the water, saying my name, holding my dead hand until the paramedics came to tell him that there was nothing they could do. I watched from my perch on the bank near where the road and the bridge met as they loaded my body into the ambulance. No sirens. No hurry.

From the gloom under the bridge, two fireflies blazed.

That was on July 10, 1987. I haven't seen my father since then. I mean, he never had a reason to come down here except to spend time with me. I guess I hoped that he'd know I was still here, somehow, but...I understand. I do.

Sometimes I'll see someone that reminds me of him. I'll sit on the bank with them, watch them cast their lines, listen to whatever advice they have for their kids. Sometimes it makes me too sad, so I'll just walk the banks, and remember all the good days before my last.

It was worse in the beginning, before I still really understood what had happened.

Maggie was the first of the others to show herself to me, the first to speak to me. She had come out here with a man she'd been seeing. He was too old for her, and her parents and most of her friends didn't even know about him, but that was all part of the fun. They came out here that night—September 22, 1975—and he slit her throat, then disappeared into the dark.

Within a few years, the man became two different people—boyfriend and maniac—and Maggie's name was lost, forgotten, and the only thing the world remembers is the same story that a million other kids tell about a thousand other bridges. Maggie is still here, though. A lot of people come looking for her (or their version of her), and she sits at the spot where she was murdered and waits for them. Sometimes she touches their cheek or whispers in their ear, and they scream and run back to their cars, scared but giggling.

There's also Henry. It took him a while to warm up to me, but now he's like the older brother I'll never have.

When the two cars full of happy prom goers collided on the bridge on prom night in 1959, they weren't going much faster than the posted speed limit. But they were going fast enough to send Henry, who was sitting in the middle of the front seat of the car coming from Bowie, clear through the windshield. All of his friends and everyone in the other car walked away.

Not Henry. He stands in the middle of the bridge every night at midnight, and waits for people to see him in their headlights. When they do, he runs towards their car while their brakes squeal and they wet themselves knowing they've seen something but not knowing what. Sometimes they'll stop to see what it was. Sometimes. They never look too hard.

There are plenty of others here: the unfaithful wives, the kids that wouldn't stop kicking the backs of seats, the husbands with the backhands that wouldn't quit until they did. They stay to themselves mostly. Mostly. Waiting.

That's the thing about Governor's Bridge: underneath all those campfire stories, there are real stories, true stories. There are real people. What is left of real people. Dad used to say the truth is always right in front of you, if you just open your eyes. Dad was right about a lot of things.

Elizabeth is still here, too, of course. No one talks to her and she talks to no one, because there is nothing to talk about. Everyone knows Elizabeth's story. In a way, we're all her guests.

Jeremiah Falstaff was appointed colonial governor of Maryland (because all the sacrifices *had* been made) just a few weeks after he murdered the maid who had helped him make his deal with the devil. He held the office for less than ten hours before he died choking on a poorly prepared piece of beef. No sooner had his dinner companions realized he was dead than his soul was stumbling up that old back road towards that bridge to meet his final fate.

All he did when he killed Elizabeth was bind himself, and his children, and his children's children, to her. Jeremiah had many affairs that produced many children, though he knew almost none of them.

Those many children had many children, and so on. Elizabeth remains under the bridge, holding the gates of Hell open to welcome each of them, just as she promised. One by one, they die at the end of lives plagued with inexplicable bad luck, and their souls march towards the bridge, shuffling from the same direction Elizabeth had come on her last ride, no matter where they actually died.

The bridge starts its metallic song when they step on it, and then time stretches out like gum pulling off a hot sidewalk, and those firefly eyes rise up and bring their great wave of damnation crashing down on Jeremiah's descendants, pulling them down to eternity in a dark riptide, while me and Maggie and Henry and the others can only pace the banks or watch from atop the truss.

I haven't been out of sight of the bridge since I died. No one has. We've all tried, but everything just circles back on itself. It's a gravity well, and everyone with the bad luck of dying within its reach is stuck in it as long as Elizabeth sits there waiting for the end of Jeremiah's line.

The march of souls slowed to a trickle and then stopped altogether for several years. Then, one night, Daryl, Greg, and I came up to the bridge looking for proof of ghosts. Elizabeth just sat there as she does in her darkness, staring, the gates wide open and ravenous behind her.

On three goofy kids still a year from the first wisps of facial hair, Elizabeth smelled the last drop of Jeremiah Falstaff's blood. In our dumb curiosity, we passed close enough for her to snatch the last trace of her murderer through the gates. If she had, the gates would have closed, and everyone would have been free: Maggie and Henry and the others to whatever their beliefs had promised them, Elizabeth to her own infernal reward.

That didn't happen, of course. Daryl got off his shots and snapped us all out of it. When Elizabeth realized that I was not a Falstaff in name or descent, it was too late to do me any good. We were all stuck, waiting for an end that might never come.

Then a few weeks ago, Greg made his trip up the road. He was the first person that I knew when I was alive that I've seen since I died. I was sad to see the shade of my old friend, but there was also a flash of shameful joy. The gloom took him in, but the gate stayed open. He was no longer the last. A fresh round of despair sent us all back to our favorite quiet spaces.

But our hopelessness didn't last long. The boy that's been coming to the river since Greg was swallowed up isn't much older than I was, and he is his father's spitting image. He comes alone, closer and closer to sunset every day, making videos with the same old camera his father had used all those years ago. Trying to bond with his memory, I'm sure. It doesn't matter. It would have come to this in the end anyway. This way, he'll just miss a few decades of not knowing why nothing he does ever seems to work out.

Hannah's Bridge

William J. Donahue

Oma never would have let this happen, Hannah thought. God damn the woman for dying too young, or at all. Seventy-seven years had been a decent life, Hannah guessed, but she had always assumed, or maybe just hoped, that Oma would live forever.

Tears obscured Hannah's vision as she cut across a meadow abloom with wildflowers. The silhouettes of the Adirondack High Peaks made soft shadows in every direction. How peaceful it must be up there, atop those mountains, away from down here, away from Mom and her wretched boyfriend, away from broken syringes and cigarette butts strewn across the kitchen floor, away from the messes made by people she was supposed to trust.

Her body ached in places she did not understand. No one had taught her that people used each other and cast them aside, as if the things they did meant nothing, as if the things they did were normal. Oma had told her more than once that the world was not such an awful place: "It can be mean and nasty and hollow and sad, but it's a beautiful place if you know where to look." Hannah wished she could still believe it.

If only she were a bird—a warbler, a jay, a regal raptor riding the updrafts—she could escape all of it. She wiped her eyes with the back of her hand and told herself to stop being a child.

"Quit being thirteen," she said under her breath, realizing how ridiculous she sounded, and how cruel the world was to expect so much of her at such an early age.

She passed through the unfenced backyards of the houses on the primary road that led travelers through town on the way to someplace else. A brown-and-white mutt barked as she cut through Mister Stanton's yard. The dog darted from one hedge to the other, yanked off its paws each time it reached the end of the rope to which it was tethered.

The grass gave way to patches of bald dirt. In another fifty feet the treads of her sneakers touched asphalt. The road led to Ausable Rim Covered Bridge, one of three covered bridges within ten miles of her home in the town of Lin, New York, nestled in the foothills of Adirondack Park. A tidy historical marker with gilded lettering described the bridge's particulars: Howe truss design, a hundred and forty-eight feet long, built in 1887 to replace a predecessor that had been washed away in an epic flood four years earlier, built upstream of Historic Lin Falls, which plunged twelve to fifteen feet over a series of drops and slides.

Long shadows suggested she had another hour of daylight left, ninety minutes at most. Oma had always told her never to stay out after dark, or if she did, at least not to linger at spaces frequented by other people. But Oma had been dead for nearly a year, and no one else would care if Hannah broke any so-called rules. Her mom had other things on her mind—the stuff she put in the needle that went into her arm, mainly—to concern herself with something as trivial as where Hannah was when the sun went down.

Hannah had other reasons to not stay at the bridge too long. She loved the look and feel of it, the way its shadow painted the cobalt-colored water as the creek passed beneath its span, the oil-and-evergreen smell as she entered its cave-like mouth and stepped from one plank to the next. But she also thought of the span as vaguely sinister. One of her classmates, Kelly Anne Simpson, had always tried to scare her by talking about the woman who hanged herself from the bridge's sway brace—"Lonely Mary," per Kelly Anne's horror stories—with an eleven-month-old baby clutched in her arms. The way Kelly Anne told it, the baby had survived the fall when the noose snapped Lonely Mary's neck, but somehow tumbled through a hole in the deteriorating spruce boards and tumbled into the waters below. The creek swiftly filled the baby's fragile lungs, dragged it to the bottom, and, later, sent its bloated body downstream for a somersault over the falls.

"Drowned, dashed against the rocks, picked apart by turtles," Kelly Anne liked to tease in a sing-song lilt, and each time Hannah's mind conjured the same crystal-clear image: a mud-brown snapping turtle retreating for the darkness of the creek bed with a macerated baby's arm in its mouth, the flesh still new and mottled pink.

The spirits of Lonely Mary and her turtle-eaten baby had haunted Ausable Rim Covered Bridge ever since, according to Kelly Anne, though she had not been the only one to say so. Apparently, several people had died on the bridge since its assembly, or at least within a stone's throw of its trusses. The young boy who slipped and fell on the rocks, the swift current taking him to his doom. The drunk motorcyclist who crashed through the wooden fence at the bridge's southern entrance and cratered in the creek at sixty miles per hour. And, just last year, the young couple who made good on a suicide pact at the bridge's center—pistols placed in each other's mouths, his and hers, triggers pulled on the count of three.

No roadside placards commemorated such tragedies, and Hannah had seen no news reports or tangible records of those who lost their lives at the site. To her, the absence of such proof just meant Lin's sheriff, mayor, and other people in power had become far too proficient at hiding the bad things that happened within Lin's borders.

Hannah approached the bridge from its northern entrance and lifted a foot onto the wooden fencepost. She squinted into the setting sun, from her vantage point a small orange ball just inches from dipping below the western horizon. The sun's rays felt weak on her skin. A chill rose from the cooling asphalt and the churning waters of the Ausable Creek. A family of four sat on the slippery rocks, laughing and sharing snacks. A mother, father, a boy about Hannah's age, a girl no older than four—out-of-towners, most likely, stopping over in Lin for vacation. Hannah gave a cautious wave that went unnoticed.

She turned and faced the bridge's cavern. As she stepped onto the first plank, the bridge's ancient smell filled her nostrils. Timbers creaked and groaned beneath her. Coldness gripped her body, the interior dark as night save the dying sunlight trickling through the wafer-thin seams between slats and the sole mid-span window facing the sun. Her presence roused a bird from its nest in the braces above. Wind from the beat of its wings caressed her cheek.

Oma came to mind, as she often did. Oma had kept two African Grey Parrots, Sammy and Deano, both of which flew through her house without constraint. Hannah recalled one of the two times she had lived with Oma for extended periods while Mom was off trying to "clean herself up," as Oma put it. Hannah would be sitting at the kitchen table, spooning Raisin Bran into her mouth, and one of the parrots—Deano, most likely—would land on her head and perch there until she finished her breakfast. The first time it happened, Oma appeared with her smartphone and snapped a picture. Hannah had laughed so hard she nearly choked on a raisin.

After Oma died, Hannah asked her mother what had happened to Sammy and Deano, but her mom gave no answer. Likely Mom had either sold them for money to funnel back into her arm, or she just opened the door and let the birds fly away.

Deano and Sammy were likely dead, Hannah realized. At the very least they were alive but desperately unhappy because they no longer had Oma around to care for them.

Hannah knew the feeling.

As she traversed the length of the bridge, a gentle wind came in from the north. She turned on her heel to return in the opposite direction and heard a distinct crack, like a gunshot, or a heavy rock hitting a wooden slat.

Or the sound of a neck breaking with the snap of a noose.

The mental image of Lonely Mary dangling from a rope made her want to run back home and hide in the closet. The only thing stopping her was the realization of what she would find, and who she would find when she got there: Mom gorked out of her mind in her bed, leaving her bastard boyfriend Lucas to ransack drawers for things to sell or, worse, go looking for Hannah.

Life was not supposed to happen this way, she lamented. When Oma had dropped Hannah off at home after Mom completed her most recent stay at rehab, Oma told Hannah to "go for a walk while me and your momma have a talk." Instead, Hannah scurried beneath the porch and listened as the women told each other what they had to say. They took turns calling each other bad names, and at one point her mother called Hannah a bad name—the worst cussword someone could call a female—which made Oma lose her mind.

"Some days I wish I never had you," Oma had told her daughter.

"Must run in the family, Ma," Hannah's mother had replied. "My problems started the day that little bitch came into my life."

Oma had died just three weeks later.

Hannah would never forget what her mother had said. She wanted to hate her mother for having spoken such vile words, but more so she hated herself for the possibility that her mother had been right.

She thought of Lonely Mary and the baby in her arms. Of the pain Lonely Mary must have felt that made her want to end her life in such public fashion, of the horrors she must have experienced, of the coarseness of the rope fibers as she tightened the noose around her throat, of the thoughts that must have gone through her mind the moment her feet left the ground, as the noose clamped tight and the world went dark. Hannah could not help but wonder about the baby, too. Had it been a boy or a girl? Had it been a good and quiet baby, not colicky, or had it caused as much trouble as Hannah had apparently caused simply by being born? The natural progression of thought: When Lonely Mary had chosen to end her life, had her decision to take the baby with her been an act of love, to save the child from the tortures the world would visit upon it, or an act of hatred, vengeance, or, worst of all, indifference?

"She was probably just a crazy lady," Hannah said, her words small and lost in so much space between the bridge's floor and ceiling. "If she even existed at all."

A baby's cry echoed behind her. She turned to see nothing but an empty bridge, the walls shrouded in darkness. The cry came again—more distinct this time, closer. She ran toward the two windows at the center of the bridge, one facing east, the other facing west. She poked her head through each porthole and scanned the waters below. On the eastern side, she saw it: a baby's arm caught in the crook between two jagged rocks.

"Oh my god."

She ran to the end of the tunnel and looked to her left. The family she had seen lounging and laughing on the rocks had left. After the briefest hesitation, she slid down the embankment and splashed into the shallow water. Its coldness shocked her, the water icy even in mid-June. The water rose to her knees, her thighs, until she reached the convergence of the two rocks. As she stared into the nook where she had seen the baby's arm, she saw nothing—just water flowing through empty space.

Her eyes returned to the bridge. Through the window she saw a pair of feet in black Mary Janes, with nothing but air beneath them, the shoelaces of one shoe undone. The feet twirled in a slow circle, as if the dangling body turned in a gentle wind. A baby's cries echoed from inside the bridge. At first it seemed like the normal cry of a baby in need of feeding or changing. Then the cry morphed into a choking, gurgling sound, as if water had spilled down its throat and filled its lungs. Hannah covered her ears with her quivering palms.

The cries stopped as abruptly as they started. Other than the creek burbling past and the cry of a loon from a nearby lake, Hannah heard nothing. A strange peace overcame her.

She realized she should be terrified by what she had seen and heard, but she felt comforted. Lonely Mary's suffering must have been too great, too profound, to have died with her. Instead she had found a way to return, to linger like a scent or a memory, as a navigator for others who came to this place seeking answers, if not a way out.

Lonely Mary was trying to tell her something. *Yes*, Hannah thought, *a clear path forward.* If things got bad enough with her mom and the malignant boyfriend, she could always follow Lonely Mary's example. Head to Ausable Rim Covered Bridge, heavy rope in tow, and loop the rope around the highest brace. *Just to see what it's like*, she told herself, *to see if it feels right.*

Oma's voice interrupted her thought: "A life well lived is the best revenge."

Hannah had once asked Oma if she had ever experienced "bad things." Oma replied easily, talking about growing up in Lawton, Oklahoma, with little food for her and her two brothers to share, through stifling summers and bitter-cold winters. Her eyes teared up when she talked about her youngest brother, who at five years old had succumbed to poliovirus.

"That all makes sense," Hannah had said. "But have you ever had to deal with things you couldn't really explain?"

Oma had paused for a moment.

"The cruelty of men and boys," she had replied. "But listen to me, Hannah: If anything ever happens that doesn't make sense to you, if anyone—" She interrupted herself, her lips pursed in a tight grin. "Well, you just tell me and we'll deal with it right quick. Life can be tough for anyone who has to go through it, and you have to be stronger than the obstacles the world puts in front of you."

Hannah felt a mix of shame and gratitude. Oma may have left the earth, but her words would live forever in Hannah's mind. If Hannah ever needed Oma, she had no doubt her grandmother would be there to intervene, to steer her away from anything that might endanger her life. A pang of guilt weighed on her like a stone. How fortunate she had been to have had someone like Oma in her life, whereas Lonely Mary likely had no one. She shook her head to chase the thought away, because guilt served no purpose. Besides, she shared none of the blame for the awful things the world had asked her to endure.

Hannah trudged out of the creek, her soaked shoes forming puddles on the dry rock. After she ascended the embankment, she took one last look at the darkened bridge and vowed never to return.

She stopped at a small garden bordered by river rocks, and lifted a steel-gray one from the mulch bed. Its edges smoothed by a lifetime in the water, the rock fit neatly in her palm—the perfect size and weight, she figured.

With a cleansing sigh, she started her return journey through the backyards, to the path that led her across the meadow, its wildflowers tousled by the wind. Within minutes she would have to walk back through her front door and confront whatever was waiting for her inside.

Her fingers tightened around the rock as she pictured the ghoulish face of Lucas, her mother's boyfriend. She swung her arm forward, as if hurling a baseball, again and again until she got the motion right. Another image came to her: Lucas prone on the kitchen floor, a pool of blood slowly encircling his head, while Oma's ghost whispered in Hannah's ear, urging her to find her mother's phone and call someone who could come and finish what she started: removing Lucas from her life.

Bats circled overhead, gorging themselves on mosquitoes and other buzzing pests. The High Peaks framed the western horizon like blackened teeth.

A baby's gurgling cry echoed in the distance. Hannah did her best to ignore it.

Acknowledgements

Cry Baby Bridge marks our fifth release in the *collection of utter speculation* series, and we are excited to celebrate this special anniversary collection. We never could have done it alone.

From the beginning, we had access to the original artwork of award-winning watercolorist Patricia Allingham Carlson. This privilege allowed us our stunning covers from the very first collection of utter speculation. We at Spec Pub would like to take a moment to remember Pat, who passed on September 10. She was a lovely person, artist, teacher friend and mother. It has been a joy working with her and we are forever grateful. Thank you, Pat.

A special thank you to Jody Robinson for her gorgeous photographs and Suburban Life Magazine for featuring our growing enterprise.

Thank you to our partners for their unending support with everything Spec Pub and the constant and unwavering love and encouragement from our children. Our gratitude goes out to Chris Bauer, Don Swaim, Ethel Jean Deal, Bill Donahue, Melissa

Sullivan, Natalie Dyen, Valerie Zell, Di Freeze, John Schoffstall, Winyah Bay Publishing, the PA Chapter of HWA, and Amy, Laura and Chrissy for their constant and continued support. We appreciate all of you.

Speculation Publications would like to thank all the writers who have trusted us with their stories. And the authors who have collaborated with us since we went official last year.

Lastly, we thank you, our readers. Some of you have been with us from the beginning, in 2019, with our first release of *The Lost Colony of Roanoke.* Some are just discovering our utter speculations. We are honored to have you along for this exhilarating journey of creative discovery and speculation.

Last of all, we want to give our shout out to Dan Kinter, always in our hearts.

-Susan, River and LC
The Spec Pub Team

ABOUT THE AUTHORS

Ray Daley was born in Coventry & still lives there. He served 6 years in the RAF as a clerk & spent most of his time in a Hobbit hole in High Wycombe. He is a published poet & has been writing stories since he was ten. His current dream is to eventually finish the *Hitch Hikers* fanfic novel he's been writing since 1986.

Ef Deal is a poet, an editor, a freelance video editor, and an author of science fiction, fantasy, and horror. She began writing at the age of 9, teaching herself to type on an Underwood Royal typewriter. Her short fiction has been published in numerous online zines and print anthologies including *The Magazine of Fantasy and Science Fiction, Dangerous Waters* from Brigid's Gate, *Beach Shorts* from Speculation Publications, and Chris Ryan's *Soul Scream Antholozine.* She is currently assistant fiction editor at *Abyss&Apex* magazine, and video editor for *Strong Women ~ Strange Worlds.* Her novel *Esprit de Corpse* from *eSpec Books* is the first in a steampunk paranormal romance series set in France, featuring the gifted Twins of Bellefées. Ef lives in Haddonfield, NJ, with her husband and her chow chow. She is a member of SFWA and HWA.

William J. Donahue is an editor, feature writer, and kitten foster. His novels include *Burn, Beautiful Soul, Crawl on Your Belly All the Days of Your Life*, and *Only Monsters Remain* (summer 2023). He lives in a small but well-guarded fortress in Pennsylvania, somewhere on the map between Philadelphia and Bethlehem. Although his home lacks a proper moat, it does have plenty of snakes.

River Eno Vegan, Herbalist, Editor, studying the occult. Author of Urban Fantasy *The Anastasia Evolution Series*. Her corporeal shell resides on the East Coast in one reality while her brain travels to alternate realities daily.

Derek Heath is a British horror author whose stories have appeared in anthologies from *Eerie River, Wicked Shadow Press, Skywatcher Press*, and *Voices From The Mausoleum*, as well as *Illustrated Worlds Magazine*. His first non-fiction piece is soon to be published in *Haunted Magazine*. Derek's first two novellas are available now and he plans to release two more—*Endless Living Organ Massacre* and *Drop Bear*—before the end of 2023.

Jean Jentilet was born in Annapolis, Maryland and currently resides in North Carolina at the whims of a miniature pinscher and a Shih Tzu. They occasionally grant her leave to write dark fiction and take long walks. Jean attended law school next to Edgar Allan Poe's grave, which was her favorite thing about law school. She has short stories featured or forthcoming in *ParABnormal Magazine* and the anthology *The Monsters Next Door*.

Dori Lumpkin is a queer writer and storytelling enthusiast from South Alabama. Their work has appeared in Diet Milk Magazine, Ram Eye Press, and is forthcoming in many other places. They love all things speculative and weird, and strive to make fiction writing a more inclusive place.

Jeff Provine is an English prof in Oklahoma, where his research focuses on folklore. He has published several collections, including *Haunted Oklahoma* and the worldwide *Compendium of Creeps*, and leads ghost tours to relate spooky history. In addition to nonfiction, Jeff writes speculative fiction and comics. In 2023, Jeff's story "Stealing Buttons" won "Most Badass Steampunk Heroine" in the University of Maryland Quantum Steampunk competition.

Brent Salish is the author of the techno-thriller *First Tuesday*. After a long and successful career in technology and law, he now writes full-time in the San Juan Islands of Washington State. He has published three business books under another name.

Cat Voleur is the author of *Revenge Arc*, and a full-time horror journalist. She lives with a small army of rescue felines who encourage her to create and consume morbid content. In her free time, you can most likely find her pursuing her passion for fictional languages.

Speculation Publications

Check out the Collections of Utter Speculation

The Lost Colony of Roanoke

The Jersey Devil

Lady in White

The Dancing Plague

And our other Books

Incubate: a horror collection of feminine power

Work in Progress: Story Crafting Notebook

Beach Shorts

www.speculationpub.com